MW00582947

STAN

marream krollos

meekling press 2019

Meekling Press
Chicago, IL
meeklingpress.com

Printed in the USA.

Cover photo by Marream Krollos

ISBN 978-1-950987-03-0

Library of Congress Control Number: 2020930427

Stan is dedicated to Sidney Goldfarb. Had anybody else been the first one to read the first pages of this book, it would not have been written.

Can I have a long island iced tea?

Can I have a long island iced tea?

May I have a long island iced tea?

May I have a long island iced tea please?

What do you want to have for dinner, Baby?

When are you going to come home?

What did you say?

I've been waiting for you to come home.

What are we doing for dinner?

All right, now what would you be if you were a dessert? You can choose any dessert, it doesn't have to be a cake. You can even make up a dessert. I am not sure what you would be either. I would be mixed berry puree. I would be pulpy purples, blues and reds. Yeah, you can eat it with a spoon in a bowl, or on a plate, or something like that. It is not stupid. Just imagine your insides. What dessert do you see? All right then, what was the first humiliating thing that ever happened to you? Come on, I would tell you about the first humiliating thing that ever happened to me. Let's see, what is the first humiliating thing I can remember? There are too many of them all bunched up together right now. I can't quite piece together what the first humiliating thing would have been. There are a few incidents that I could say happened early on, but which one really matters? That is, which one matters enough to be called the first one, the one that led to all the other ones. Which moment humiliated me enough to be that? The first humiliating thing could be any one of the first humiliating things that happened. Don't worry, it will come to me. No, don't worry about it. I want to know too. I want to make a list. I will name it The List of Humiliations and hang it up above my bed in the room. Each humiliation will be numbered and next to it will be the age and season during which it occurred. This way I can remember all of them all at once instead of being reminded of each one individually throughout the day. My best friend says that a list like that can help a person understand who they are. It can tell you what you are. You should make one too. Then maybe we can read each other's lists and get to know each other better.

I know I felt humiliated when I got on a train to surprise my best friend who lived far away. No, it couldn't have been the first time I was humiliated. I was twenty-one. It was winter. She had said that she had been too stressed out to call me. That's why she couldn't be there for me, because she was too stressed out about work and bills, and I wasn't being understanding. I wasn't being there for her. She said I put these emotional demands on people who are only trying to live their lives. She said I want too much from people who are trying to get things done so they can live, so they can be happy. But all I could think about while she was explaining this to me is what if I needed you because I had been raped, would you call me then? Would you still be this steely when you apologize, if you apologize? Would it be all right for me to call you crying in the middle of the night if I had been raped? But every woman I have ever loved has been a steely apologizer, I suppose. They don't usually feel as sad as I do about us not talking, or not apologizing. They don't have to, maybe, they don't need to talk or apologize as often as I do. They don't worry about whether or not there will be anybody there for them if they ever get raped. I get really sad when a woman I love doesn't love me because only women have ever said they love me. I always have a best friend who loves me until she feels I am being demanding, then she doesn't know what to do with me anymore. I do cry and cry on the phone sometimes. It would be difficult to listen to all that crying and still have time to fuck your boyfriend. Anyway, I got on a train to go visit her. I couldn't afford a plane ticket, so I was on a train for three days going and three days coming back. But when I got there I had to listen to her with her boyfriend every night. It was insensitive of her really, especially considering that I had not ever had a man. She knew that. Listening to her orgasm made me wonder how stressed out she really had been. My best friend and her boyfriend always said things to each other while they were fucking. You know I only call it fucking because I think there should be only one word for it. They would say things to each other about how much they loved each other and things like that. I mean, I assume it was about how much they loved each other. Sometimes it seemed as if they were talking about how their day went, or what books they have enjoyed lately. It was hard to understand every single thing they said, the talking went along with the incredibly loud fucking noises. He would make high-pitched grunting, injured animal sounds. She would scream as if her baby was about to run out into traffic. It was this squealing, squeaky noise that she made. I could still make out that there was talking going on, though. I kept thinking, I wanted you to call me, and you are my best friend, and you didn't call me even though you knew I was all alone. You have somebody to talk to and fuck every night. I borrowed money to get on a train. I hate being on trains, she knew that. I slept sitting up for days to get here. Knowing that speaking to me on the phone while I am crying is not as important to my best friend as fucking her boyfriend made me feel unimportant. It humiliated me. It always does humiliate me, when women I love would prefer to fuck men they love rather than hear me cry. And when I feel humiliated I cry. I cry like nobody cries. I howl and shake. I make strange squealing, squeaky noises. These noises usually happen because I can't breathe right when I am crying. I make these interrupted choking noises as if somebody has their hands around my throat while they are pounding away at me. I will also at times make these strange riding a roller coaster screaming noises. Eventually I feel a little better. I reach that orgasmic level of release, eventually. Then I can fall asleep, and wake up again. So she was with her boyfriend, who was saying things to her while they were fucking, and I went in the other room and howled. I cried for the earth. I often cry for the earth at various times, for various reasons. I know you think crying for the earth is cliché, but so is everything else. That particular night I thought about how the pitiful planet earth cannot escape from this strange relationship she is in with the sun. And she cannot escape because she has people to think about, she has responsibilities. She is stupid. She is a train that wants to drop all of her people off somewhere but never gets there, never finds it, so she chases herself around and around. When I wake up, I thought, they will have stopped fucking and the earth will once again have completed one trip around herself. She has once again already done everything she will ever get to do, but is still waiting for something. The people are heavy, thirsty, tired, but she does not know about cycles, she believes everything goes in straight lines. She is ignorant and stupid. She thinks she is flat. She does not know what she is. And to make matters worse, as more people get on board she feels as if they are coming closer and closer to reaching her stomach, to sinking into her gut. So she constantly feels as if she is nervous even when she is not. She always feels as if she is falling. She spins bit by bit without realizing anything is spinning. I bet the earth wishes she could just die and go to hell already. Hell for the planet earth would be to be released from her orbit and fall into space. She is afraid of constantly feeling as if she is falling though. She doesn't realize that it would be very similar to how she feels already as she spins. And she does not know this, because she does not know she is spinning. She knows what it feels like to spin but she cannot make lists. She does not have any way of figuring out what she is. This is really what I was crying about while listening to them fuck. I sounded like my mother does when I make her cry. I tell her that she is too stupid to really love anybody when she tells me she loves me. I let her know that she is a stupid animal and she can't love like other people can. I know, you thought that I was crying because I don't like to hear people fuck. You thought that I don't like to hear people fuck because it reminds me of how I don't have anybody to fuck. You think I am petty and jealous. That's what my best friend thinks too. When I asked her why she didn't come in to hold me when she heard me crying she said she didn't come in because she didn't hear anything. So I told her everything that happened to me that night and she said what do you want me to do, what do you want from me? Do you want me to just be alone because you are alone? Why can't you just be happy for me? Why can't you just be happy for your friends? I am not petty, I said, I was really just thinking about how the earth is spinning. I was thinking about that drunk beggar I saw in an alley when I was a little girl walking down the street holding my mother's hands. He was spinning around and around under one street light, arms outstretched. I was young, but I knew already that nobody really had anything to give him. No, not really. I wanted to tell him he could just slit my throat if it would make him happy. He could cut my face if it would make him feel better. I wanted to say, I know you are hungry and sad, so if it will make you feel better you can just kill me. Since I was rich compared to him, he was poor compared to me, so taking my life might have soothed him, I thought. The power of being able to take is soothing. So I hope you can accept this gift, I would have said. Kill me. Take what we all can take from each other, from me. We can walk in on the sleeping and interrupt their sleep for a single moment before we take everything from them. What is potentially mean about this is that it is done without knowing if we are even giving them anything in return. But then again we will all die anyway. You should just be able to do it once, take everything you can see from somebody. We can also lie down with others so we can make a life, but I could not have known that then. And there was probably nobody who would have fucked the drunk old man, because he was lonely and ugly. If there was I could have said, you too have the power to kill a rich child, and the power to bring one more poor child to the earth, Sir. I would have said this if I had known that then. I didn't say any of these things to the drunk man who was spinning like the earth, though. I instantly realized that as he got nearer and nearer to my throat I would have thought I don't deserve this. I have never really been that happy and if I have never been all that happy then I deserve to live on, and grow up, to have a chance to be somebody someone wants to fuck, even if cutting me, or raping me, or killing me would make him feel powerful. And as I thought about all this, it happened, my quickly formed friendship turned into a silent emotional struggle between me and the drunk spinning man. I started to wonder whether or not the man was mean, whether or not he deserved to be poor. Some people really only think lies are mean. Or is it ignorance some people think is mean? I think people are mean. My best friend says that people are not mean. We just don't always understand each other. I think meanness is something that doesn't change, no matter how long or how many people get on board the earth. Whatever it is that causes rape is what I think is mean. Whatever it is that made all those people put all those people on the trains. Some people will have you believe that it is ignorance, or lies, that cause rape. But they say that because they are mean too, but they don't want to admit it. I know, because I pay attention to these things. I am very interested in murder and rape. But I am interested in rape only because I am sure that after you have been raped you know what it means for people to really be mean. I believe it would be the number one most humiliating thing to ever happen to me. You know we are something bad when you see a person pounding away at you as if your body is made up of the water you stole from them. They are parched now because of you. It's all your fault. They must want my water back, you start thinking. But, it is my water. I can't live without it. This doesn't make sense, they are trying to go in and suck my water out of me. They can't live without your water either, though, that's the problem. That is why it gets so complicated. You have to come to terms then with how we, people, are mean and figure out what you are going to do about it. Would you still reach for most offered hands if you knew that most people really would stand on your face just to raise themselves up a bit higher off the ground? Would you put bread in your mouth in front of people who would let you be put on a train if it could keep them from being put on a train? Once you have seen meanness for yourself you have to stop thinking that you can be happy in this world because of people. You have to base your good and bad days on something else. You have to base them on how mean, or not mean, you are. Because all sins are not created equal. They are very unequal in fact. They come in big and small. The biggest sin, in my opinion, is forcing someone into living, forcing them into being born without them having specifically made that request. But, taking a life and making a life is what makes us feel powerful, so we do it anyway. My best friend says that life is a gift. I think the biggest sin must be bringing someone into this world without them having given you the permission to stick them in meat. So it is not fucking that is the biggest sin, not exactly, but the occasional outcome of

10

it. My mother didn't think about how fat my thighs would be, or how they would call me Humper in school, or how I could possibly be raped. She did not ask me if I wanted a fair or dark complexion. If somebody doesn't want to be here then life is just a prison and they are on death row, literally. The saddest part is that now that they know what it is like to be stuck in their own meat they are scared to leave it. It is all they have ever known. It is a lose-lose situation they are in from that point on. We all have to forgive our mothers before they die though. They are animals too. Biologically, they must make and save, thoughtlessly. My best friend says we are animals with social constructions. She's right. She's always right. My best friend is one of those people who can tell you anything you want to know about life. You only have to have a conversation with her for a few minutes before you understand what life is all about. I think we all know we are not supposed to be here. She thinks I am wrong. We all know we are not meant to be animals, if only because we feel we are not. So, we search for those who would have us believe we are wrong. Give our lives meaning, so to speak. We travel from what a person says and does to who we think they are without any real evidence. We assume someone is kind, thinks we are worth the meat we are encased in, that someone will take care of us, because they paid for the meal. They laughed at the joke nobody ever gets. They could have gone home right after they fucked you, but they didn't. They stayed and fucked you again. We have to do this, assume things about others that we would like to believe are good. We know that otherwise we may be very alone for a very long time, and we don't like being alone. Eve assumed that Adam was a good man because God made him first. When he blamed her for the eating of the apple she was already under the assumption that he was good, so naturally she assumed she must be bad. And Adam either ate the apple because he trusted Eve, or he believed he must have trusted her since he had already eaten the apple. That is if an Adam and Eve existed at all. They may have not. But my best friend says that we are all very religious whether or not we believe in an Adam or Eve. But if you don't believe in any type of a spirit world at all then you can at least explain away the rape and murder stuff with biology. You would still have to wake up not knowing what will happen to you from one day to the next, but whatever happens, you can then explain it away with biology. You can remind yourself that animals rape each other too. My best friend is an atheist. She doesn't believe in anything and she still thinks life is a gift. To be a real atheist would require kamikaze strength of character. You have to go through all the motions of living knowing full well you are only wormfeed. These people know that they will remember nothing dead, be nothing dead, so they are really nothing now, yet they keep on living, these people. They know that the people who say they love them are only saying that because of biochemical reactions that make them say things like that and they still keeping on living. They can have orgasm after orgasm while their best friend is crying in the next room. They dive into life like slick, graceful, killer swallows without a purpose. A true, good atheist, like a snake, would only think to hiss when it senses danger, would only be hungry when it has no bread. I suppose it doesn't matter either way really. Either way we only come to love the people we are supposed to love. You know what I mean, children and wives, or even cousins sometimes. For most people it is the case that if they didn't know their children were their own they wouldn't be able to stand being in the same room with them. My best friend brought up once how differently we treat somebody when we don't know they are related to us. If you take into account how many people fuck other people who are as old as their children are, or would have been, then it becomes obvious that there is no real connection between age and any sense of protection we may have for other people. I, for example, have fucked an old man. I was twenty-four at the time. It was summer. And I wouldn't have done it if I knew you then. We were good friends, before the fucking started. After talking to my best friend about it I realized that I really only wanted to feel befriended and loved, but he wanted to fuck. You see, I am dark and the old man was very fair. I was young and the old man was old. Being dark and young made me appealing to the old man with fair skin, made me worth fucking. How many times have you heard some old man say, yes, but she's very mature for her age? No, she doesn't have to drink herself into a stupor to fuck me because she is grossed out by the thought of being with me physically. She has shown up at my door drooping, drunk, and willing ever since I told her I don't just love her as a friend, ever since I told her that I cannot just be her friend. She is so mature that when she realized she would have nobody to talk to if I stopped speaking to her, because I could not just be her friend, she decided to drink a lot and fuck me. Yes, that's how mature she is. I don't really know what the old man was thinking, but he was right, I really was just lonely. He had a daughter older than I was by a few years. He did not love me like he loved his daughter. I had to give him something to get love in return. That is why everybody gets all fussy when somebody risks their life for somebody else who isn't their child, because we are obviously only supposed to love our own children, when we know they are our children. I heard a story about a woman who threw her body down to save a little boy from being attacked by a dog. It was a story people told because it was somebody else's child under her body. She gave her body to the boy. She wedged her body in between the boy and the angry dog. That was strange. That seems selfless, but because of biology we now know that it isn't. But we are an unusual species of animal, if not a selfless one. My best friend says that there is nothing that is usual, or unusual, in nature. But I think if there is life somewhere else on a distant planet and they are watching us then they must be confused by now. First of all, their planet doesn't spin around like a woman trying to save her children. It stays still like a man waiting for a woman to get up after he has pushed her down. They won't attack. They can't attack until they figure out what makes us so upset. Unless nothing makes sense there either, then they are fine with us doing the same things for different reasons. The whole idea of sense might not even exist there, but if it did then they would really be confused. I wonder what they are saying about us right now, don't you? You be one alien, I will be the other. Come on, just for fun. Please. No, it is not stupid. All right I will do it all by myself. I will be both aliens. One of them is watching thinking I do not understand these things. What are they doing here to each other? Then the other one says, oh, this is what they do to each other. But why do they do this to each other? This is how they multiply. This is how they multiply, but one of them does not seem willing? Yes. Why? Haven't we figured out that it gives them pleasure and power to multiply? Now we believe it may not always give them pleasure, sometimes it takes pleasure away from them.

How can a pleasurable act not be pleasurable at different times, do their bodies change accordingly? We believe that it is not their body that it injures in such instances. They do not like knowing that they are on a planet where pleasure can be taken from them if they don't want to give it. Do they all do this to each other sometimes? No, we don't know yet what makes some of them do it and not others. Some of them have it done to them but do not then go on to do it to others, some don't experience it themselves and they do get pleasure out of doing it to others. And this over there, is another one of them upset? Yes, another one of them is upset about how soon they will turn to dirt. Have we found out anything new about why they seem so unwilling to turn into dirt most of the time, but then turn themselves into dirt sometimes? Yes, they are not always scared to turn into dirt, in fact sometimes they are more scared to stay in their meat, but if something tries to turn them into dirt then they feel they are being taken from, and they don't like it when others try to take things from them. Have we found out anything new on why they will sometimes turn themselves into dirt to keep somebody else from turning into dirt if they know they will all turn into dirt anyway? Yes, at times they are more scared to stay in their meat without the others they have known than they are scared to turn into dirt. But we still are unsure as to why that woman got on top of that boy to keep him from being eaten by a dog.

Maybe the most humiliating thing to happen to me was the first humiliating thing to happen to me which was when I was twelve and boy number one said I looked like a dog. He actually said that it would be insulting to dogs to have me compared to them since dogs are not as hairy and ugly as I am. We were all waiting in line during gym class in our green shorts. I had just said the words: that is an ugly dog. So he said you should be talking. You are even uglier than dogs, he said, and went on to explain the hairy insulted dogs bit. But I had seen him sitting on a bench and his eyes were as brown as a desert. His eyes were so brown that I loved him. I came to believe that he was better than I was and that I was undeserving of him. So if he liked me then it would give my life meaning, so to speak. Apparently, he thought I was undeserving of him too because he later said to me, you shouldn't even be talking about dogs. It is an insult to dogs to compare them to you because dogs aren't as hairy or as ugly, or something like that. He said it in front of everybody standing in line. Some people laughed. I walked home from school that day and a couple of his friends threw little rocks at me. They were calling me a cockroach. Cockroach didn't stick, Humper did though. They called me Humper because I was born in a desert and camels are born in the desert. Camels are born in the desert and they have humps, and the only animal that would hump me is a camel. Get it? Only a camel would hump her. Humper. My best friend says that they didn't like me because I was the ugly, hairy girl who dared to like the boy with beautiful brown eyes. I was the girl who did not realize how ugly and hairy she was, or what it meant to be hairy. That was humiliating. It happened in the fall. Ten years later boy number two was supposed to make it all better. He played the guitar, he had beautiful blue eyes, and he had an accent. He had an Irish accent. He had a beautiful Irish accent. It made everything sound so beautiful, as if he and I were in a happy cartoon together. All of this made him even better than the other boy. So I loved him. He was really, really the first person to kiss me, even though four other people had had their lips on my lips before him. He kissed me the way I would kiss myself, the way my pillow kisses. But I felt undeserving of him and he felt that I was undeserving too. That's why he said that I was begging when I wanted him to stay that night and sleep next to me. But he let me give him my head to make up for it later. Then he pretended to be sleeping, so I would leave his room. I use the term, to give head, because there is not one word to use for it. And it did feel as if I was giving him my whole head. I have given my head though, and I do think there should be just one word for it. A year later boy number three was supposed to make it all better. He was an awkward, tall boy. He was very tall and very awkward with red hair and blue eyes and I felt that he was undeserving of me, but that he would not think that I was undeserving of him. So I thought this should be the first boy inside my body. Immediately afterwards he threw my underwear in my face, and a few hours after that he told me that he had a woman named Judy who challenged him. I don't challenge him, he said, although I was the better listener when compared to Judy. A year after that boy, boy number four came along. He was really going to make it all better. He was tall and he was very deserving of me and made me feel as if I was deserving of him. He was funny and not awkward. This made me think I was funny and not awkward. But then he said to his friends that he fucked me because he thought nobody had done it before. About one year later I fucked the old man. This was an old man who had a wife who was mean to him. I knew there was no way this old man could make anything better, but by this point I was really lonely. So, I fucked him because I was really lonely. His wife had told him that his penis was too big, his breath smelled bad, and his hands were too clammy. Those are the words she used, penis and clammy. My best friend says that I wanted to make him feel deserving of somebody, since I felt undeserving of everybody, and he was my good friend whose wife made him feel ugly. He was ugly, and I am ugly, so we were ugly, or we are ugly. We really loved each other though. The next boy, boy number five, was repulsive in every way. He was an awkward human being who talked about small women being bent up like pretzels. I am not small. My best friend says I fucked him to feel disgusting. I wanted to know what I am. I wanted to rape myself using him, to show myself what I am. That's why she can't feel all that sorry for me. This other boy, boy number six, was in a bar one day. He said he wanted to spend the three days he had left in the country getting to know everything there was to know about me. In the end, he figured he knew enough after just one night. Boy number seven was in a bar one day too, a sailor that fucked me in a park. He called me Baby, just so he could fuck. The next boy said I might as well walk around with my legs wide open because I come off as just that big a whore. That was my problem at the time. Apparently, I gave off this vibe of being wide open. So I spread my legs wide open for him. He is the boy who said I was The Master though. Why? Because I kept saying, I want to feel you inside me. Don't put it on because I want to feel you inside me and I want you to feel being inside of me. That's how I became The Master to boy number eight. But he still wouldn't sleep next to me. I save that for people I care about, he said. Please don't leave, I will feel like a whore. I save that for people I care about, sorry. I had to go find somebody who would sleep next to me. That's when I met a really nice, awkward boy who seemed to really like me, so he must have been even nicer, more awkward than I thought. He said he wanted somebody to give his life meaning. A year later there was the boy who doesn't remember, boy number ten. He woke up and he could not remember what happened, so did anything really happen with that boy? If a boy fucks in the middle of a forest but nobody hears him? Then there was the boy who did not have time to be anything to me but the ugly, awkward, yet sensual boy who wanted to kiss my whole body, including my ass, as I shook in fear of what could come out of my ass the whole while. The next boy was a nice, awkward boy who fucked me because I said I would fuck him after he insisted he wasn't trying to fuck me. He had to fuck people like me because no-body had ever told him how to wear his pants so that he does not look awkward. Boy number thirteen was a factory worker who had only fucked two other people and didn't like kissing women down there. He would not give a woman his head. He said it would taste bad. His friend had given women his head and told him they tasted salty. He asked me how many times I orgasmed every time that I never orgasmed, ever, when I was with him. He would ask, how many times did you come, and I would say, a couple. This is mostly because I don't orgasm when fucking men. I am sorry to have to let you know this way. The next boy was my man. He

21

could have been my man, anyway, if he had wanted to be. He didn't, so you don't have to be jealous. He didn't want to be anything to me, and I wouldn't have wanted him so much if I knew you then. And then there was the beautiful boy a year later, boy number fifteen. The boy who was beautiful. The day after I was with the beautiful boy I woke up and I realized that I have hair on my stomach. I have always known this, I suppose, but what I realized really is that he may not have wanted to fuck me again because of all the hair on my stomach. I remember complaining to my best friend about the hair on my stomach. She tried to make me feel better by telling me that she has hair on her stomach too, but her boyfriend still kisses her there. It's ok, he still kisses me there, she said giggling. It could have been the hair on my stomach, or it could have been that he had to tell me that something was coming out of my nose. Do this, he said, as he mimicked nose wiping. I had to clean out my nose in front of him. I wiped my fingers on the carpet. It could have been that I am not good in bed. He said I use too much teeth when I give my head. He made jokes about not being able to walk in the morning. It could have been anything. As I gave him my head he said, just move your head, stop moving your whole body. But it had to be something because he didn't fuck me again, and I wanted him to so much. Beautiful boy was not nice or awkward. If he had been with me again I could have possibly believed that I was not just nice and awkward either. Beautiful boy was not as beautiful as you are though, so you don't have to be jealous. Somewhere in between boy number one and the last boy is the other beautiful boy with an accent. He made me feel funny, which is not like being nice or awkward, but he thought I was too something, fat or something, I couldn't quite put my finger on it. And the other beautiful boy with an accent, I asked him to teach me how to say butterfly. And the beautiful boy with an accent who never showed up that Tuesday afternoon. And the boy who saw me naked only once and didn't call again. I saw him later in a room where everybody was drinking and asked him why he never called. He took me to a corner where it was more quiet and said you should shave, down there, you have too much hair down there. Shave. Just shave.

Could all of this humiliation possibly be because of Adam and Eve? They are, after all, our first example. These two people, a man and a woman, may have had to fuck their own children and let their children fuck each other so that there would be human life outside of heaven. Then one of their sons killed the other one because he was so lonely that he wanted God to love him as much as God loved his brother. And then the people put the people on the trains. But what really should matter to us now, as you and I consider the various forms of humiliation we have experienced and

23

make lists, is whether or not my cunt smells bad. I only use the word cunt because the sound of the word cunt is what a cunt looks like, and I need to use only one word for it. No, those other single words for it do not sound like tunnels. Stop it. I just don't like the sound of the other words for it, they don't fit as well. Anyway, it does not smell bad all the time, whatever you want to call it. That is to say that I work at cleaning it well enough to be able to safely guess that my cunt may not smell bad all of the time. In a world where a lot of people don't wash properly down there I have something to be proud of, I think. Some of the boys I have given my head to needed to wash better. After boy number two stopped talking to me his friend came to the room and pushed my head down on him. He said suck. Suck. Just suck. I said but I will feel like a whore. He said you aren't a whore you are just lonely. He was trying to be nice. He had not ever washed down there though. Lots of people who are not awkward or nice, and so are beautiful, don't smell good down there. It might change things if we all knew just by looking at somebody who did, or did not, smell bad. It would give us a different set of reasons to be proud of ourselves other than just being beautiful, or ugly. And pride is what I think matters most to us when it comes to this boy and girl business, because it all boils down to avoiding humiliation. You have to take each other's clothes off, meaning you will have to smell things, meaning smells are important. It should really matter more than how somebody looks, if you really think about it. But it really isn't what matters most to people and that is why my best friend says I am very sad sometimes. And being sad is, of course, why I am still without you. Nobody will love you unless you can first love yourself, all the people say. People will feel that you don't love life and they won't love you because you don't love life. It makes sense. We are all looking for reason to believe that we should be here, to give our lives meaning, so to speak. If I seem sad all the time, about being here, then you will start thinking, maybe I am not meant to be here either and you will get sad too. I know. I know I should just be happy just like she says. But I can't do anything except have strange fantasies all day and all night. Because if I stop having the perverted fantasies at night then I won't be able to hold on to my pillow after we have had a fight and say come on, Baby. Stop it now, Baby. Come on, Baby. Let's just go to sleep. I love it when my pillow and I have just made up. I wouldn't be able to keep from howling about some humiliation or another that was brought to mind during the day unless I was waiting to get home so I can get in bed, reach over and hold on to my pillow and feel my legs shaking. I wouldn't be able to get in bed and feel my legs as they take each other slowly under the covers, wonder about how my fingers could have mastered the doling out of the perfect amount of pressure so soon.

They have only known me for years, I think to myself, and they know me so well already. I need the fantasies and a pillow. Pillows, when you hold them, become whoever you want them to be. Otherwise I would need you to kiss my hairy stomach once every night and you can't always be there to do that. You are a man, so what would I say to you if I had you in the room on my bed? What am I supposed to tell you, that my whole life is the story of a few minutes with my father? Really, those were all stories about a few minutes I spent with my father, Sir. My father, who is not really even a man himself, who is a boy, who is really just a sad baby, is why I say and do all these things. He is why all these things happen to me. At least that's what she says. No, I don't want to be happy, I would say to you. No, not really. This happened and then that happened. Now will you just like me, or respect me, or something? Is that what I would be saying to you if you were in the room? No, we should just lie in bed and look out the window instead.

Why do you say these things? You know that it is not that I don't want real kissing. I want to be happy. I want real kissing. Kissing pillows is better than real kissing in many ways, but it is heavily based on the idea of real kissing and comes with its drawbacks. I don't like how often I have to change my pillowcases first of all. I don't like how sometimes I get fibers from the pillowcases on my tongue. It is better than kissing pictures on walls though. That was really hard, my thin lips, sticky against paper, my lips grating against my teeth. I spent a lot of time kissing walls when I was younger. My best friend would leave me in the room alone to go be with her boyfriend. I would get drunk, put some music on, and pace around the room and kiss the walls. I stopped when I found out people could see me through the window. I still do it occasionally though. If I am pacing around to music and suddenly in my daydream you are kissing me, then I will just throw myself against a wall and let it take me. Of course, I want real kissing, but the thing about real kissing is that most of the time I like it done slowly and softly. Most of the time I want somebody to put their lips between my lips slowly and softly. Sometimes I would want the man kissing me to repeat one slow, soft movement a hundred times before moving on to the next thing he will do slowly and softly. Sometimes I would want to want the man I am kissing so much that I cannot smell, or taste, or judge his breath properly. I want you so much that smells don't matter. The thing about kissing is that if you are doing it tenderly then you must feel something for the person, and if you don't feel something for the person then you can't do it with any type of sincere tenderness. All this would lead us to the conclusion that good kissing doesn't come without the feeling of something for the person, which comes with the fighting about something with the person. Nobody wants to fight with me. Nobody thinks I am worth fighting with, not even you. That's possibly one of the very basic ways people are different. Some of us want the kissing without the fighting, and the rest of us want the kissing without the fighting too, but we go about getting it in different ways. If we love each other so much, and we do everything together, then we will fight and make up because we will be in so much love and we will make this love the most important thing ever, one of them thinks. But the other one thinks if we don't really know each other then maybe we can get together sometimes and kiss and there will be no fighting. But then you will make me feel like I am just a whore, the first one says. Well, what do you expect from me? What do you want me to do about it? What do you want from me? It is not that anybody wouldn't appreciate taking a cold shower with somebody who doesn't like cold water. Your naked body against their naked body, with baby streams of water separating into strands against you, in between you. One of them, shivering slightly, says I hate cold water. I don't know how you can be in water this cold. The other one pulls the cold one closer to their body and whispers in their ear, it will feel warm soon. Or the way wet hair feels against your hands, like hair is made of skin and tissue. Or how good water tastes once it has been running down someone else's mouth, once it has been mixed in with their water. Nobody really minds that part of it all. What they do mind is how you then have to pay attention to the person you have done that with just so they let you do that with them again. You want somebody to stick around so you can do things that felt good over and over again. This is it, and it is all very hard to carry. My best friend says that love is like a good lie, once you speak it you have to make sure you won't give yourself away with anything else you say or do after that. That's why if I were to ever want to kiss a man only once, I would want to kiss a good man, not a nice or awkward man. I would want to kiss the man who would think that the crazy looking person sitting across from us on the bus, the one hugging his bag of groceries, is the most beautiful thing he's ever seen. The milk, the soup, the crackers, the bread will be safe with this strange looking socially awkward human being, he would say to himself. He would turn his head slowly and softly say to me that this bread is going to make this man feel safe. The white, white milk is like water. It will go down his insides through his mouth smoothly and outline him from the inside. He will drink the milk from a cow and eat the grain from the earth because he, like us, is an animal. We are animals. But we put food in these pretty bags and boxes and label them with bright colors because we are people too. How beautiful it is that everything makes sense now, the man who I would kiss would say to himself. When he is lonesome, this beast of a man, he will reach for the milk that is safe in his home, that will be safe in his body, and he will not worry. The milk will not walk away. It will fill his mouth when he is sad. It will slide down to line his tunnel. The white water will not go anywhere until he is finished with it. And this man who I would kiss, because he thinks these things, would say about me to his friends, I am falling in love with her. Why do you love her, they would ask him. I love her, he would say, because she's been waiting to die her whole life. And her voice always sounds like it is crying. She can only whisper or scream but in both cases her voice sounds like it is crying. She scribbles by going over letters again and again, not by drawing circles or hearts or stars. She knows I know she's ugly and she doesn't care, because it doesn't matter to us. Her cunt smells like soup and bread, so I have to love her. She makes me realize that I am supposed to be here on the earth. She gives my life meaning, so to speak. Could I then tell him that I have considered what it would be like to stab a person in the ear with my pen just once? Would I be able to communicate that type of curiosity to him? I have sat across from a man who I did not know before and wondered could I possibly take this pen and put it deep in his ear. I wondered this because I do not know the meaning of life. What if I had taken the pen and buried it in his ear, what would have happened? If I had kept pushing it in despite how the pen resisted and how the man's face resisted? What would have happened then? The man fighting, flailing with his arms outstretched, and me pushing and pushing with the pen. Would all the water in the man leave through his ears? Would the earth stop spinning for a second to give people a chance to notice this new thing? Would it be something new? Would everybody in the room be annoyed that they have to stop and pay attention to this man only because he was stabbed? They would have to pay attention to him and they don't even love him. Would they move their bodies to hold the man or be still, angry with the man? I might have ended up being the one who got all the attention out of that situation. He would have to force attention out of the people, that pitiful stabbed man. I mean, how can something that strange and horrible happen to you without you deserving it somehow? If he didn't deserve it then it could have happened to me, the people would think. I would not have to beg for attention. I would be famous. They would give me a name. The Crazy Girl. Sometimes you just have to do these things so you can know what you are. The only person I ever really thought I could say all those things to is you. You are the friend of my best friend. I think you are good, not just nice or awkward. You asked me what I wanted to drink and I said can I have a long island iced tea. I don't remember if I said please. I listen to it over and over again trying to hear myself as you heard me. Can I have a long island iced tea? It's no wonder you don't love me. I always sound as if I'm crying. Everybody hates the sound of their own voice on tape though. There is hope still that I sound beautiful, but will never know it. I have to hear myself say many different things in many different ways before I can really judge my own voice, before I can really know how I sound.

You walked around for a while, put brown water in a glass and gave it to me smiling. I saw your fingers around that glass filled with water a color similar to the shade of my skin. I imagined your hands on my skin. So I talked about how much I would rather fuck you than fuck those stupid red tulips standing in rows outside with all of my friends and your friends, with the hope that word will get back to you, of course. I thought somebody should know how much I want you, Stan. Because when the whole universe realizes how much you want something it gives it to you. But you have to let the universe know that you want it enough for the universe to give it to you. Eventually, God or a friend will tell Stan about how I feel, I thought. Someday a friend of Stan will go up to Stan and tell him about me and my love for him. Stan, you made her feel as if there was a soft tunnel inside her that went from the space between her legs all the way up to her mouth. You made her open up from the inside, from the space between her legs to her mouth. A tunnel opened up where you should be inside her, Stan. Two parts of her where you could exit and enter, exit only so you can enter again. You could come and go as you were filling the space between her legs with your cock and tongue, up to her mouth with your cock and tongue. God needs to use the word cock only because that's what you call it. You made her feel that there was a hollow tunnel inside her that needed you. She had to turn the red tulips into you that night, Stan. She wanted to take the red tulips and stuff them inside her. She wanted to slowly put them down her throat through her mouth, slowly put the tulips up in between her legs, until the tunnel was filled with tulips that were soft petaled like you. She imagined you larger than you really are so she could be small underneath you and have to feel nothing but you on all sides. She imagined you larger and larger until she could walk and stumble on your skin, burying her whole body inside the scented corners and bends of you. She walked on your body like she walks on the earth, without being able to see the end of it. Then she imagined you so much smaller than you actually are so she could take you in her hands and put you whole in her mouth. You became something she could put in her mouth, Stan. She let you soak and wilt there until you entered her bloodstream through the soft tissue inside her cheeks. She took you out of her mouth and slowly put you whole in her cunt. Her whole body shivered softly. She imagined you small enough for her to be able to feel your whole naked body with one stroke of her tongue. She wanted a dozen whole Stans crawling up and down inside her tunnel. But I know that neither a friend, nor God, is going to be willing to help me like that. Tulips don't live for very long anyway. They all die. One minute they are opening and closing slowly, softly at the edge of your half open mouth. One minute their petals are softly stroking your lips as they are drinking the water that is dripping out your tunnel. The next thing you know, their petals are moving further and further away from you, and from each other. They begin to look as if they are being tortured. Their limbs are being pulled away from their bodies. Then the petals, having been stretched so far away from each other, brown, wither, and fall.

When I see you I just smile and stare at you. I give you this creepy look as if to say I am a woman who cannot use her body, a woman who cannot, even if she wanted to, feel her cunt. I do not orgasm with men. You will be the first one to make me orgasm, Stan. Don't worry, I don't really care all that much about what happens with me and you in the future. I just wish I loved you and you loved me. I wish that I had you because I think that if you were mine you would appreciate little, cute love notes I would write you. I would write on a little piece of paper, I want you every time, every where, every thing. But I accept the fact that you don't want me. I just think if we ever could be together it would be nice. I can really imagine you watching me put lemonade in my soda and thinking that it is really cute. I can see you being surprised by the discovery that all soda tastes a little better with a lot of lemonade in it, and feeling as if you learned something about the pleasures of living from me. I can see you realizing how much you missed out on by not knowing me for all those years, and wanting to make up for all that time by knowing me forever. But it doesn't really matter to me. Don't worry. You see, despite what she says, the only way to really be happy is to not care about what happens to you. So you are all right with being hungry. You are all right with being cold. You are all right with being raped. You are all right with your children being raped, after they have been murdered even. You are happy to be on the train. How do you do that though? You would have to pretend you wanted everything that happens to happen all along. You would have to pretend that you wanted everything that happened to you to have happened to you the way it happened to you. The same way I pretended I wanted to fuck that boy, boy number five, the one who kept a dildo in his drawer to fuck himself with. It was really easy to do that. You would have to try and feel that it is only ever a good thing to have something inside you, no matter the reason you happen to find yourself with something inside you. Everything would have to feel good all the time no matter how you got to it. But what if while you are being raped somebody just happens to be walking by and they see you there in a corner, under one street light, arms outstretched under a man. They stop and stare for a while and you look up suddenly and unintentionally you say, help me, in a whisper. What if despite yourself you find yourself whimpering and whispering, help me. Please, I do not really want this. Help me. I was just pretending to be happy so I could be happy someday and then somebody could love me. That's the only reason I was not trying to fight this man off of me. But now you have passed by, Sir. So, I would appreciate it if you would help me please, Madame. They would not believe you. Look at how slowly and softly he is fucking her they would say. And that's wonderful. If they helped you it would ruin everything you worked for instantly and you would not get to say that you were a happy person before you died.

I know all about death because my uncle is dead. That is uncle number two, he is dead now. My family met in different hospital rooms for a while. First my family met up at holidays and birthdays, then at weddings and births, and now we will only meet at funerals. We don't cry when one of us dies because we are all old enough now to know everybody dies anyway. We meet and try to forget how often we have been mean to each other. I would hold my dying uncle's hands sometimes and he would grab my hands back, but I would forget that he can hold hands for a long time and I would let go of his hands too soon. He would be hurt by this, even though I do everything I do to be kind. I would see that even the good in me is nice and awkward during those moments. We come together to try and remember how long it is that each one of us could hold hands before letting go. We left each other even after we had figured out how often each one of us was right and wrong. After we discovered that we all sometimes know some things and sometimes we do not know other things. We left each other because no one watched what had been and wanted it to continue. That is why now I have you but I am without a family. But I said goodbye. I stood by my uncle's bed and thought Uncle, I am thinking now about the mean things you have said to me, and I am also thinking about death and how it doesn't really matter what you said now, but maybe it still should. Death should not be so bad that it beats pride in the end. It should not win, especially since it is so common. Pride is what should matter most to me because in the end I believe it will keep me from being lonely. But then I would remind myself that his body felt the lumps on other bodies and got pleasure out of knowing what those lumps felt like to be touched. He did this with his wife and I do this to pillows, but we are the same. The lumps of our body, the lumps on other people's bodies alone make us family. So I would think, you have a right to be sad and lonely right now, Uncle. Because you are dying. I am sorry about the things I have thought about you. I understand you right now because if I were dying I would expect apologies too, since all my life I have apologized so well.

I sometimes say to myself, you have a right to be sad and lonely too. Especially since it is often dark and breezy in the room and we are more often than not alone in it. It seems as if someone's arms would make this better, doesn't it? But don't be fooled, I scream at you. Just because it is cold and dark blue outside and it feels like you want arms around your shoulders, or hands on your back, does not mean you should have them, Stan. I know how the weather gets sometimes and how it makes you prickle all over, makes you want to be tamped down. Arms are never the right thing to want though. Think about all the things you do have that others do not have instead. Think about how lucky you are. I always tell myself how lucky I am. It does not always work. For example, I tell myself, you are not on a train. You can sit here in the cold and dark and wonder whether those people on the trains enjoyed the view from those trains. Those trains traveled through some beautiful parts of the earth. The people must have seen some very lush forests. And there are other beautiful things they must have seen. Did they think about the nature of trees then, those people on the trains? If trees are what God made for them to stare at because they are beautiful and make people wonder about him? Did they know that trees would be the last bit of God they will ever see? Except for, perhaps, the beauty of human blood. The blood of the human being, which I believe is darker and thinner than animal blood, often spills to let us know we are killing, or that we are ourselves dying. It is an alarm system that often fails us. When those people on the trains, who hadn't drank for days, asked for water and the soldier finally let them have some water, they were so happy, because of water. They were still on the trains, but they were suddenly so happy. Then the soldier spilled the water just as they were about to drink it and laughed. Did they think then why is this happening to me? Why is this happening to me? I am a good person. They might not have known how to be happy in life. They might not have realized that you have to expect everything and accept everything and see the good in everything and pretend you wanted it all along. But they just kept thinking, why is this happening to me? I know they did. I know they did because I know about death now. And because that's what I thought when I couldn't get that bottle of water to come out of the vending machine that one morning. It took my change and gave me nothing back, I thought. Why is this happening to me? I am a good person. Surely the meanness in other people makes us assert our blame-less goodness even more violently than the meanness of a machine does. What would actually be nice about surviving something like being on a train though, is that you could get respect afterwards for having sur-vived something that the people agree is horrible. You would not have to be told by your best friend that you don't get to talk about rape, because you don't know what you're talking about, because you don't actually remember what happened for those few minutes. For example, if a bomb explodes in the room and I survive the fire, the flying concrete, being buried under rubble and other potentially horrible moments, then I get to be special. Or do I get to be special? Do you have to die to get the respect you deserve for having been through something horrible? That would be easier. That way everybody who respects you doesn't have to listen to you. I would get to say I survived this horrible tragedy, but would you only be impressed if I had died in it? What does it take to impress you, Stan? What I know would not impress you is my cunt. No, not the inside part, the whole outside part of it. Yes, there are separate words for each part of it, but I want to use only one word for it. Remember? I hope you would not mind it too much though. All those boys did not like my cunt, and that is all there is to it. The boys thought there was just too much of it. But what can you do? What could I do differently while getting to know intimately somebody who does not like my cunt? I was born that way, so what can I do? I say this to myself. I then wonder why we judge so harshly these things that we think are bad, things people are just born with, while we fuck them. Why are we so mean, I ask myself. I try not to do it. I notice things, but I remind myself that if I feel as bad about them as the boys have felt about my cunt then I will be a hypocrite for feeling bad about how the boys have felt about my cunt. If I feel bad about what others have thought of me, then I should not think bad things about others. If none of us can help being a certain something then why would it bother any of us? But still sometimes I find myself staring at somebody and feeling disgusted by them. This is how I know that I am mean too. If for no reason at all I can be staring at somebody who was born with their skin or their nose this way, or their eyes that way, and I can feel disgusted, then I am mean too. That is how meanness works, my friend says. It is more random than ignorance or lies. It is at first random, then devises its reasons. The pimples looked like they were all about to burst, or the nose took up his whole face. I should have been disgusted. I deserve it, I am a good person. That's why I told her that I know I am evil, and so I want it to hurt me. I want every thought of every man who has not believed I was the most beautiful girl ever to lie naked on a bed, or in a park, to burn like a cigarette being put out on my eyelids.

On your skin, bumps would be pleasant places for lips to stop while on a trip down your body. They would be there to mark the terrain of your face, or your back. If I had you I could forget about all this. If you loved me, if you thought I was beautiful, and you thought my cunt smelled like soup and bread, I would never think anybody, or anything, was disgusting again. And I would not have to resort to needing that fantasy anymore. If you thought I was beautiful then I would not need those strange fantasies. Especially that fantasy where I have a boy who has a best friend who is dying and has never fucked anybody. He wants me so badly before he dies because I am so beautiful, and he's been waiting for somebody as beautiful as I am to fuck him. So, the boy arranges it so we three are together. He loves his best friend and completely understands how horrible it would be to want me so desperately and not have me. He arranges it so that I can lie down and have one of them inside me while the other one whispers in my ears. They are saying something about how beautiful I am. One of them whispers while the other one is giving me his head. They take turns. My boy does this out of love for his best friend, who wants to die having had me, and who is not at all awkward or nice. You are nice, but you are not awkward. You would make everything better. You have brown hair and brown eyes and I would believe everything you have to say. You do have brown eyes. We can't be too sure though, can we? Eyes do come in different shades, as does hair, as does skin. There are many gradations of hair color in different populations. Hair color is interesting that way. If you start with black hair, which would apply to most people in the world, then the shades of brown, then blonde, then red, then you eventually get to auburn hair which would be the least common hair color in any population, and so the most special. This really awkward boy I knew when I was twenty four had black hair like most people on earth do. In many other ways he was like most people on earth are. I did not really want him. I let him kiss me and it humiliated me. It was winter. I liked how he wanted to kiss me though. How he wanted to remember how I let him put his mouth on mine once while he was drunk, as if I were special and he undeserving of me, as if it is something good to kiss me. This made me happy because already at that point I was pretty sure that most people on earth did not consider it a good thing to kiss me. When I found one person who did he became special somehow because I could feel special when he was looking at me. I had auburn hair and emerald green eyes. That is what I would have chosen if I were given a choice before being born. I would have been kind of tall, but not too tall, with auburn hair and emerald green eyes. I actually like blue eyes more than I like green eyes, but blue eyes are more common, and so not as special. I actually hate the color green, but I would love to have special eyes. I would put a little red in your hair to make it auburn, but I don't think it would look right on you. We have to find another way to make your hair as special as you are. Yes, I know, thinking about all this, the nature of what does and does not make us special, while a man is inside me is probably why I cannot orgasm while I am fucking. At least I hope it is just about thinking too much and not that I am just one of those women. You know what I mean, one of those women who doesn't feel anything because they don't really like fucking. I can orgasm when I am alone in the room with my pillow though, you know that. Especially if we are listening to good music. I pretend that my pillow can sing beautiful songs and it makes me wild for my pillow. What do you think about this? You now know that listening to another man's voice and pretending it is coming out of my pillow could make me orgasm, though you would not. Does it make you sad or does it just make you think less of me? She is too hairy and she is not good in bed. I bet if I could read minds I would have heard that a lot, Stan. You would probably just think I have a problem. My best friend says that's what we do to each other, generally. We label people depending on whether or not they have problems, and what the various types of problems they have are. But I don't really know what you would do. I don't really know you because there are all kinds of things you have to learn about a person before you really know them. For example, how and when do you applaud when you are a member of an audience? Does it depend on how you feel about a particular segment of a performance, or do you just applaud when everybody else does? What do you take pictures of when you are traveling in a country you have never been to, and how many pictures do you take? Do you sing out loud to your favorite songs? Only when you are alone, or whenever you feel like singing out loud? How would you react if I tell you that I have been raped? What will you think if you find out that I was lying about having been raped just to see how you would react? A really good man would start crying for me, whether or not anything actually happened to me, he would cry. He would cry and cry for the earth that carries us on its stomach, and for me, because I don't remember. A good man is very different than a nice guy, Stan. A good man is not at all awkward or nice. A good man knows that what makes him good is not only how he kisses a woman but also when he chooses to kiss a woman. A really good man, like the stripper in the leopard print G-string who was at my best friend's birthday party, the police officer, would cry whenever he is sad for me. He went into the kitchen to eat cake after he had let them knead his ass. I followed him. He sat there and ate cake in a leopard print G-string. I watched him and asked him questions about his life and he responded casually. I could tell he was very kind though. I knew he also thought I was a very thoughtful, very wonderful person. Maybe he had labeled me as such, a problem-free person. I need a good man like the stripper. He could have judged me for my shyness about ass kneading, but he didn't. I think he liked me more than he liked her, even though he let her knead his ass. He felt that I would be great in bed. He could tell. I could tell that his father loved him. People think that a man loved by his mother doesn't rape women. They are wrong. A man has to be loved by his father. Otherwise he only has had love from a woman and so believes that women are the only place he can find his water. It doesn't really matter who the good man is or what he does though, just as long as I am not disgusting and humiliated my whole life like my mother. One day I saw my mother eat a tomato. We were waiting in line, waiting to get into a park so we could all ride roller coasters, and she took out a tomato and began to bite into it. Tomatoes are soft and watery. They spill. All the water inside them leaves when you bite into them. I saw my mother's face with red tinted water. I heard the sounds of tomato skin ripping. She is disgusting, she eats like an animal, I thought. These are the sounds of an animal eating. Then I wanted to apologize to her for being disgusted by her. How do you say to somebody, I watched you eat and my stomach turned upside down? You can't say that to your mother. She is, after all, the woman who would let you hold onto one of her big fingers with your little hand when you couldn't sleep. Now whenever I want to apologize to my mother silently I imagine her eating tomatoes. I imagine myself handing her tomatoes and watching her eat them one by one without looking away. I imagine stuffing tomato after tomato in her mouth and down her throat without being disgusted by her. I look at her. I smile lovingly and think, all right, we are all animals. I replace disgust with pity. Pity feels different against my chest. Disgust slithers down towards my stomach, pity waves out towards my mother. Pity makes me want to be the one person who can watch my mother eat a tomato and still think she is special. I remember the day she gave money to the man who was not begging and humiliated him. She put money in the open hands of a man who was only sitting outside a store drinking coffee. She must have thought he is ugly and does not wash, so he must be begging. She looked at me and smiled because she thought giving him money would prove to me that she was good, that she was a person, so not a stupid animal. We walked and I waited until the man couldn't see us, then I punched her arms as hard as I could. He wasn't begging, I said. You never give money to people

47

who are actually begging but you gave money to this man who was not begging and you humiliated him. You humiliated me. She started crying and making her strange animal noises. I hand her tomato after tomato.

The problem is that my mother has only ever been fucked without orgasming her whole life. And she has been all alone, for the last God knows how many years of her life, without being fucked, or orgasming. She wanted certain men but they never wanted her back. She gave them whatever they told her to give them, but they still did not want her. I carry with me those pictures of my mother reaching up with her long island iced tea colored hands to put herself on the dark skin of men who did not want her. She and her humiliation are baked in my memory. That's a great idea. I will make a list for her too. That stupid look on her face as she would reach up for their faces with her hands is stamped in my brain. She was so happy, reaching smiling. So, I either have to fuck really short people, or have to not fuck at all, or fuck only fair skinned men so that the cycle is not repeated.

You see, my mother was born in a place in the desert where they cut at the cunts of young children. So was my grandmother, so were my uncles. I was born there, too, but nobody cut at me because my mother was too stupid to arrange it. She never considered that it might mean I wouldn't fit in. I asked my grandmother while she was lying on her bed, how does it feel? She said it feels normal. How do you know that you wouldn't be happier with my grandfather if you could feel more when he was inside you? She made a face and turned her head. She usually thought I was disgusting. I feel enough, she said. But how do you know you wouldn't feel more? Because, I feel enough! So, I asked my mother how it feels while she was staring at a mirror. She explained that the part that they cut off is only the part that keeps women from walking comfortably. She said there is excess skin that dangles there and it has to be cut off, or it rubs against your thighs. I told her I didn't believe her. I told her that other women feel more than she does. I told her that I have excess skin that dangles unevenly, but it does not rub against my thighs or keep me from walking. She said, if you touch yourself you can never be happy with a man, and you will go to hell. I told her that I think a woman is happier without men if she touches herself. She said that I will burn in hell if I do it and in hell I will be alone forever. But she will be alone forever too, and she never touched herself, so obviously touching yourself is not what makes you alone forever. Only once have I thought about my mother while I was on my pillow though. I thought about how wonderful it feels to orgasm and how my mother cannot, because she does not have that little part inside her. Some people in the desert, where she and I were born, think that if you do not cut at a cunt it will grow down past a woman's legs and dangle forever. I saw myself showing her how to put her own hands in different places so she can pretend to understand how good it feels to have a whole cunt and be happy. We were alone, naked in the bathtub, water falling down on us from the shower head. We were giggly little girlchildren together. Then I remembered that she does not even have that body part there at all. She cannot even pretend like I can. Everything inside me turned to dirt. I became dirty, and so did the thought of my mother. Her soft body made me disgusted and disgusting, as if she was made entirely of mucus and my mouth was on her mucus body and I was sucking her up. So I had to think quickly about something else, something more pleasant. Men. Men and their harder bodies. Men who are waiting in line to fuck me. Old men, young men, beautiful men, and ugly men lined up in the dead of night. I am lying naked on a bed of sand in the desert where I was born. I am spread out, arms outstretched, like a yellow star on brown sand, my face towards the black sky. There are men lined up waiting for their chance to be with me only once. They have come from all over the earth. They do not do this because I am beautiful. They have heard about how I smell, how quickly I can orgasm, and how often I want to orgasm. They are so nervous they are shivering and balmy. They wait with their dewy hands wrapped up in each other. One by one they take off their pants and lower themselves on top of me. They cannot believe they get to make me writhe like this. No, not me. I am undeserving, they think to themselves.

I have to be loved. I have to be loved, which means being happy, but I don't know how to be happy without you. I don't know how to be happy without knowing that you will love me whether I am happy or not. My best friend tells me that if I am this unhappy alone then I will be this unhappy if I had you. It has to come from inside you, all my best friends have said. But what if I am an exception? What if I am the exception that proves the rule for everybody else? I may be the only one in the world who needs you to be happy. Doesn't that make you feel special?

You are tall, but not too tall, which is good because I do not want to reach up too far to put my hands on your face. You have fair skin. You have brown hair and blue eyes. Fair skinned people are a combination, a mixture, of different peoples all blended together. All those groups of people who fair skinned people are composed of today wanted to kill each other at some point. Now they stick together and want to kill other people. But if everybody not fair skinned fucked everybody else who is fair skinned then we would eventually end up having to hate each other for reasons other than our skin and hair and eyes. Or we could still hate each other based on our colors, but we would have to be much more specific about it. Or we could just want to kill each other depending on whether or not our toes are too slender. Or we could divide the world into people with wide feet and people with narrow feet. Then we would all have to take off our shoes the way the men on the trains were made to take off their pants. We would find a way. The meanness always finds a way. It is always inside us and our bodies have holes, our skin has pores. You can stop hating black haired people, but you would need to replace them with some other kind of people. You squeeze us from one end and the hate rushes to the other. All you can do is try to keep it contained within yourself. You try. You fail. You try, you fail. But this is the only way to spend a few minutes of your life not being mean. If I told you all this and you disagreed with me I would say this is just my opinion, Stan. You're ruining this conversation for me. Christ, Stan, I was just thinking out loud. Sometimes I feel like I just can't be myself around you. I would realize then that you are not the man who thinks that the guy hugging the bag of groceries is the most beautiful thing on earth. That man would just talk with me sometimes about things like the nature of evil. So I would have to scream at you to let you know that I am upset. Then you would think I was crazy because it is not socially acceptable behavior to just start screaming at people. Socially acceptable things are good, so if you are crazy you are bad. You are also bad when you are raped because you are unhappy after that. You have a problem. You are bad when you can't orgasm because it makes you bad in bed. If you enjoy fucking a lot, and let men fuck you whenever and however they want, then you get to be great in bed. You have to be really loud, too, though. It makes them feel good. You have to really get pleasure out of it, whether you are actually getting pleasure out of it or not. But if you are really enjoying it then you are extra special. Then you get to be called wild. Being wild is definitely not like being nice or awkward. Then you get to really be The Master. My best friend is The Master too. She is wonderful in bed. I heard her. She had told me, even before I heard it for myself, how good it feels to fuck her boys. She has always enjoyed being with all of them. It makes me sad that I don't know how good fucking can be with a boy. What is it that would make you moan like that, I wonder. I don't scream like that with my pillow, but I think it feels as good as fucking anything can feel. I think I feel enough. So, I asked my best friend what it is that makes her scream like that. She said it is the unexpected. You scream like that when you are with a man, but not when you are with a pillow, because you know what your pillow will do to you to make you feel good, but you don't know what a man will do to you to make you feel good until he does it. But no man has done the unexpected to me. And what about having to expect and accept everything so I can be happy? Men won't ever make me want to scream, I thought. I am one of those women. Then I felt humiliated and I cried and cried. I howled and screeched, as I do sometimes. Why do I always expect everything all the boys do? How to be surprised? How to be surprised? Now my best friend thinks I am crazy too. We cannot talk like giggly girls anymore because she can orgasm and I cannot. I am going to go be with a man, she says. No, don't go, stay with me because I am crying. Why does it matter to you if I go see a man or go see another friend? But I would stay with you if you were crying. Are you so insecure that you have to always feel like you are the better friend? She asks me this. She is so upset. Yes I do, because only women have ever said they loved me. I have only ever been a friend, so that has to be something special. But I let her go. I do not hold on to her body and scream. Stay with me! Sleep next to me! No, tonight she will sleep next to a man, I think to myself. He will contain her smaller body within his larger one. She will feel his warm, wet breath on her back one second before she feels his lips on her back. She must do this because this will make her happy. I am sad, but she is stressed and so needs this. I must understand. I am sad because I do not sleep next to men. But she must go and lie next to a man tonight to make herself happy, because

54

she can lie next to men, but I cannot, and she cannot change that. Let her go. You will sleep alone in this bed, in this room, tonight. Your chest will lovingly open up to inanimate objects. Your gnawed eyes will open and close over and over again throughout the night. She will roll into a man's chest and her face will kiss his face unknowingly, because she can, and you cannot, but you cannot change that. She will not only leave you alone right now, she will leave you alone and go to a man. She will not only leave you alone and go to a man, she will leave you alone and go to a man so she can be happy. She cannot change this. She cannot stay with you, she has already told him she is coming. But everyone cares so much about the suffering of the starving babies. That's because the starving babies have a right to want food. You have no right to want arms. Besides if she does not go sleep next to a man tonight, how would you know that you are as lonely as you are? How would you know what you are?

All right, let's try and figure this out. What would make someone scream like that? Only something that makes you so happy, or horrible sadness. Sadness could make you squeal like that, I thought. Sadness, over the loss of his best friend, made a mystic walk around and around a lamppost. The walking made the sadness go away. So, all the other dervishes whirled until they felt nothing too. You see, sometimes our meat has its own feelings that we do not take care of because we are too busy dealing with our sadness, Stan. I take care of my body's sadness by pacing too. I pace like the mystic. Sometimes I pace around my room to music for so long that I have to stop because my feet hurt. I will throw myself against a wall every now and then if there is somebody kissing me in my daydreams. I should have just paced while listening to my best friend fuck her boyfriend. If I had paced around and around I would not have cried and cried.

Now I am sitting in the room having lunch with your best friend and my best friend and some of our other friends, but you are not here and all I can think about is you. I think about all the other things I have to tell you. I want to let you know that I want to be a cartoon. Everything is so wonderful in cartoons. The colors are so strong. Color has power in cartoons. Have you ever noticed how cartoon people can fall and shatter their teeth and then get all their teeth back in the next scene? When they are knocked out they see pretty little birds and little stars. Then they get right back on their feet. You cannot hurt the body of a cartoon. You cannot take anything away from them. Cartoon people do not have to work since they do not seem to need to eat. And then you say, yes, but the sky looks almost exactly the same in real life as it does in cartoons, have you ever noticed that? No, I had not. Thank you for pointing that out, Stan. The sky is already as beautiful as it would be if we were cartoons. I see now. The sky cannot be improved upon in cartoons. Some things on earth we cannot really improve upon. No, not really. And then you ask me, have you ever noticed how we associate trees with the color green? Yes. Why? Well, in the winter trees have no leaves. In the fall their leaves are red, orange, and yellow. In the spring they are just budding. Why do children tend to draw trees as they look during only one season? It must be because we see things as we want to see them, Stan. That must be it. We like to remember things as we want to remember them and not as they actually are. We like to forget what we do not want to remember. No, we do not like to remember ourselves as we most often are. Then we secretly search for people who will see us as we do not want to see ourselves, but will still want us despite what they see, which we do not want to see. The ones who will recognize that often we are without leaves? Yes, the ones who see our branches empty, and scraggly, but will fuck us anyway.

I need to explain to you that sometimes I do not want to speak to you at all because it is always much too complicated, or much too simple, a topic that we speak about. And when I say what I have to say to you I am often considered a liar. I want you to ask me why I want to get away from you, so I can explain to you that

I will never have the hair I want and my breath will never smell like what I want my breath to smell like. I want you to ask me why I often cannot sleep, so I can let you know that it is because I think about rape and all the other reasons people have woken up to knives at their throats. I want you to hear these things and then just fall madly in love with me. If you cannot love me, because of these thoughts I often have, then I will feel unloved. I will try to change my thoughts but I will not be able to, I will not be able to change what I say. I will want you to love me for what I am now. Love me as I am. I will have lived and been unknown. Nobody will ever find out how sensitive my back is. Nobody will ever know that slowly and softly touching their lips to my back would make me wild. If that happens, then I hope you realize what you did.

Yes, right now. Now you ask me what else I want. Ask me what else I want. What do I want that is not you, you ask? I want to be a beautiful painter, Stan. I want to be a painter who paints fucking. No matter what she paints it is really, actually, just fucking. She can paint a mountain and some trees and she is only capturing the essence of fucking. She herself doesn't fuck though. She is so beautiful that she doesn't need to, you see. She can afford not to be touched at all, she is that beautiful. She is brilliant and beautiful and she is a painter. She is a genius actually. She speaks many languages.

Really speaks these languages, not just says she does like some people do. I am not just talking about conversational skills. She is fluent in dozens of languages. She is also sincere, and kind, and funny, and incredibly generous. She is a strikingly beautiful painter who is hilarious, vibrant, brave, and strong-willed. She is also a martial arts expert. She has never really even had to learn martial arts, she just has a way with these things. She beats men up all the time, men that try to touch her because she is so beautiful. And she is good with children. She is really good with children, interacting with her changes their young lives in fact. She does not try to tell them the meaning of life as she sees it. She explains to them all the different possible meanings of life, so they can choose for themselves. She doesn't want to have any children herself though. Her name is Leam Osheay. It is pronounced like the Irish man's name is pronounced even though she is not Irish, or a man. She is a native of some place very exotic. No matter where you live on this planet, this place she is from is exotic. Or perhaps she is a mixture of ethnicities that are all very exotic. Leam doesn't need to fuck, even though any man in his right mind would want to fuck her. But Leam doesn't really care if she gets touched. This makes her challenging. It makes men want to touch her. She would be amazing in bed, of course, if she ever did fuck. She is very passionate. She is an intense, charismatic, riveting individual. And what makes her cry so easily all the time is not just about kissing, or touching, or anything like that. She is just very sensitive because she is an artist. She is in tune with everybody else's emotions as well as her own. It is probably just being alive and not knowing the meaning of life that sometimes makes her so upset. Not knowing if she is a good person, though she is. She is the best person on the earth. She is not as devoted to the poor as a nun would be or anything like that, but she is much better looking than any nun. And she beats men up who try to touch her at bars. Maybe she doesn't know what she is either, but she is not weak enough to do bad things just so she finds out what she is. She just isn't sure if she is a good person, that's all. She isn't sure how to be a good person, or if it even matters at all. She is not sure if there is a heaven. She wonders, if there is no heaven then why do I do all this painting now, only to become nothing in the end? Why bother painting wheat fields, that are really just fucking, if we are only meat? If the fact that we rape each other all the time and put people on trains proves that we are meat now? If we become only our meat in the end anyway? If death turns us into meat and we all die? Are we meat that gets upset, she wonders. If fucking only makes us more like our meat then is it worth painting? It makes us happy to be our meat. It makes us want to be our body, which is only meat. We are meat that squeals. We are meat that rapes, or squirms to keep its babies from being raped, then rots. That is why we must forgive our sisters for not bearing our crosses. We must forgive our brothers for forsaking us, for not accepting their position as our keepers. We must learn to forgive all the people who have let us suffer though they too know what it is to have a father, and they know what fathers can do to you. These are just some of the conclusions about living life that Leam has come to so far. Leam keeps living, though, and she stays so beautiful. She is probably the most beautiful woman on the earth. She is definitely the most beautiful woman on the earth right now. She has black hair and brown eyes, which would ordinarily be the most common, the least special, but not on her. Her skin is similar to the color of a long island iced tea, which is true of most people in the world, but is still a special shade on her. On Leam all shades of black, yellow, and brown are spectacular. Her lips feel like they are made of many curled petals. Her mouth is a pink rose that opens and closes at will. Next to Leam's mouth my mouth looks like it is made of skin and teeth. She can't be described. You just have to see her for yourself. She is all I want, other than you.

So, I am sitting in the room with your friends and my friends and Leam. I make a joke, but it is inappropriate. I think if I keep repeating this joke they will laugh, if I keep explaining they will get it, if I keep trying I will be good. I will make them understand that it was really funny. It really was funny. I will be good enough for Stan. Leam thinks I am good enough for you already, but not the others. She wants me to be with you but you want to be with her. And my stomach has started churning and cramping after that exotic lunch in the room. So now I think, would it not be appropriate if right now I was surrounded by the stench of my rotten insides? What is inside my slimy stomach anyway? Would it not be amusing if a squealing sound announced to everybody that I was rotting already? But if I ruin this opportunity to impress them I will want one more chance. I will go back to the room and tape myself so I can figure out how I sounded and what I could have said differently. I will rehash every word that came out of my mouth and lament deeply. I will pretend that if I could just do this over, and do it right, I would not ever need to do it again. But that would be a lie. We all say we want one more chance, just one more, so that we have something to appreciate or remember. So we could just do it right, one more time, and let go of wishing we had done it right. If I could do it over I would have given my head better, we think. Remember, less teeth, less teeth. But really what we want is one more chance to do it right so that we are worth doing it with again, so that we are worth wanting again. So, I instead tell them all that I love you. I really love him, I say. I love him for what he is. I really do. Of course, they tell me to just be happy on my own. If you are not happy alone you will not be happy ever. You cannot rely on somebody else to make you happy, you have to be happy alone. I explain to them in detail why I can't be happy without you. Suddenly, everything is silent. Everybody is still. The moment is nice and awkward. I try to make things better by letting them know that I wake up everyday to find that there are no lumps in my breasts. And that this makes me truly happy for one moment because I can feel lumps there all the time. But when I use my fingers to find them every morning I find out they have disappeared. This is wonderful because I will never cut off my breasts. You think they are my best feature. My father once told my mother her breasts were the only thing on her body worth touching. My mother's breasts are my breasts. Thank God I wake up and I cannot find the lumps. I imagine the slit that is my cunt being cut into me by God before he sent me down to my mother, so my father could ask me to show him what Hanan did, and I wonder why God would do that. I am a girl, I tell them, I know some things that there are to know about boys. I know that their breath always smells better when their tongue is in your mouth than when you are a safe distance away from their tongues. That is why I would always rather kiss men who have bad breath, or men who can't like me, so that I can stop judging their breath and every-thing can be better. I know that you cannot wait for some man to be in love with you, to love some man because only a certain type of man is capable of feeling in love at all. And that type of man is not a strong man, and when he is a strong man he is not a kind man, and when he is a kind man he is not a good man. And when he is a good man he doesn't want you. I know that I can't appreciate a good fuck because I freeze when someone is inside me. I begin to think about how special I am. I freeze and wrap my arms around them so they don't notice. Then I ask them how it feels so they can let me know whether or not it feels as if their cock will explode. This is how I get them not to notice my not being special, I feign curiosity. The old man said, my cock is going to explode, when I asked him. I cried in his arms once and asked him if he could imagine what it would feel like to not be able to remember. He stared at me and said he doesn't know what that would feel like. He was trying to be nice, and I wanted him to love me, so I pretended to want him inside me at that moment. He seemed to really appreciate that. It proved to him that I was normal, that I didn't have any problems that could keep us from fucking. You are not interested in any of this, are you? I know you would be, if you only knew what you were doing to me, Stan.

I know that if you pray to the dead they intercede for you. If they are in heaven they can intercede for you like saints can. They are with God and so they can speak to God on your behalf. So far everybody I have known who has died has known what it is like to feel ugly. My grandmother was never really loved by a man. I am not even sure if my dead uncle, her dead son, ever really loved her. She married a man who sometimes thought she was a good wife and sometimes thought she was a bad wife. My cousin who lived most of his life in a wheelchair knew what it was to feel ugly too. He wanted so badly to be kissed all the time, and then when a woman who wanted to kiss him all the time finally came along, he died. My grandfather was never loved. He was married to my grandmother. He only cared about whether he had a good or bad wife. This made my grandmother not love him, even though the woman she wanted to be most was a woman who only wanted a man to think she was a good wife. If I pray to these people who have died I know they will intercede for me and God will give you to me. If I say Grandmother, Grandfather, Cousin, Uncle, I am so sad without him. Sometimes I don't know what to do about it. I cry and cry. I pace and pace. I tape and listen to my own voice over and over again. I know you never felt loved too, and you know how horrible it is. Would you please ask God to make Stan love me? I know one of them will ask God for me. Then God will whisper to you about me and you and the red tulips, and you will regret having ever spent a day without me. You will want to make up for it by staying with me forever. I will pray to them. Maybe they cannot do anything about me and you. Maybe there is nothing even God can do about us. I will pray to them anyway, because they may still be able to tell me what heaven is like.

Who gives this woman to this man? God does. God gives me to him. Who will walk me down the aisle when I marry Stan? My brother says it will be my father, but that really hurts my feelings. It really does. Why did he say that? I will never know. I will never know. My brother and I watch each other. We are both strange animals that the other is watching. I think my father didn't really even want to fuck me, and my brother doesn't care. He doesn't care about who does or doesn't love me. I think my brother has overheard me talking about the room with my mother, and he still doesn't care. I know I remember the room. I remember telling my father I had a secret to tell him about my cousin, whose name, Hanan, means kindness, tenderness, gentleness, softness. Do you want to know what Kindness did with a boy? What she did with a boy or with a man? It was a man. Of course, you have to tell me. So, we had to go to a bed. This way we could lie down next to each other and my father could put his arms under my head. Then when we were lying on a bed, just like Hanan and the boy, my father asked me about what Hanan and the boy were doing to each other. I told him what I had seen with my very own eyes. I told him what I saw. Hanan didn't have any underwear on. Show me. She had her underwear, but it was not on her body. What do you mean? Show me. You have to tell me everything that happened. I even have to show you some of it. I have to reach to take off my underwear and my father has to reach to help me. I know this because I remember my legs going up higher and higher so that the underwear could come off, because it wouldn't come all the way off when I was lying on it. So, I proved to him that I had seen something special. It is possible to take your underwear off while on a bed with a boy. That is what Hanan did. I am not lying. No, I am not lying. How did she take her underwear off? Show me how? After a few minutes, now that I know what happened, he thought, I am going to leave the room. Should I put my underwear back on? Put your underwear back on. All right, I will stay on the bed and put my underwear back on and you can just walk out of the room. Now put your underwear back on, now. I put my underwear back on. Then I remember leaving the room and pacing. If I had a radio I would have listened to music too. I did not know what to do now that I was not talking about what Hanan did with the boy. What to do now? What to do now? Walk around and around a pole. For a while my father thought I was a good person because I had told him a secret. I hope he doesn't tell Hanan. I made him swear not to tell on me.

Yes, my best friend thinks there are reasons to believe there may be a God. The first one, sometimes my best friend just doesn't feel like she will ever die even though she knows she will die. Sometimes she feels that she loves people who biology has told her not to love. She loves poor people, and dirty people, and people who are not beneficial to her survival. Sometimes people reading cards on a table, or lines on her palm, tell her what has happened to her and she wants to believe them even though she knows about science. This all means there is a God. Yes, Stan, there are also reasons to believe there may not be a God. We act like we are all evil, but that doesn't make sense, so it may all just be biology. We cannot see a God. We try to speak to God and we hear nothing, unless we want to hear something. We know all about biology now so it is stupid to believe in a God. We know about chemicals and evolution now. You see, Stan, a long time ago ape-like animals needed chemicals to convince them to love so they could survive longer, better. One of them had this mutation in her brain that made her think she was willing to fuck even when it was not her mating season. This made the other one of them stay with her to fuck her again because it was easier than waiting alone. Their baby ape-like animal survived longer because its mother wanted to fuck its father all the time because of a chemical mutation in her brain. According to biology, this is the first almost human baby to have a real father. That is why now people love each other and want to fuck. We love and want to fuck, proof there is no God. Mothers ask God to save their children and the children do not get saved. This is proof there is no God. Children die, but even though their mothers know that they would have died anyway, and that they will die anyway too, they still feel sad. This is proof there is a God. And most of us living on this earth are just too hungry for life to have any meaning other than bread. It is true, Stan, most people on the earth right now are hungry. If there is one true meaning to life then it would have to be the meaning for everybody on the earth, but all the hungry people don't care because they just want to eat. The meaning of life cannot be bread. No, it cannot be just bread. Arms are important too. All this must mean there is no God. But if there is a God and he went through all that trouble to give us stars then he must really love us. Just imagine all the trouble you would have to go through if you were God and you wanted to make stars for people. And you do all of this only so the people you put on one of your planets can look at pretty sparkles, and maybe see better at night too. You would have to start with one star then turn it into a solar system with one special planet in it. Then you would have to put that solar system in a galaxy of many solar systems. Then you would have to put that galaxy in a universe. All this just so the people you made on that one planet can look up at the pretty little lights that come out at night. If God loves us enough to give us big things like stars then we should not be angry at him for things like rape. He might just have been so concerned with the big details that he overlooked some things that could happen to some of us while looking up at the sky.

There's this boy, he is also a friend of a friend. I could fuck him, but I would only want to so that you can see us together and be jealous. I know you would hear about us, eventually. But really, really I would only be with him so that I could make myself cry. Sometimes remembering past humiliations does not make me feel enough, and I have to feel raped so that I can howl and yelp. Put somebody inside my body who I do not want there. So I can know myself. So I can know what I am. I am the type of woman that can be with this nice, awkward guy, but not with you. I am that woman, Stan. I judge myself as I would judge those women. It is only fair. I am not meant for a good man. I am awkward like a nice guy.

Do you know how often people give me advice about you? They say that I should just be happy. That is what I want too. That is why I want you. I want to be happy. I want to be happy. I want to be happy. I want to know if there is a God. I want to know what to do to be a good person. I want to be worth fucking to someone who I also want to love me. I want to know the truth about God and the meaning of life. I want to know what I am. I knew when we first met and I saw your fingers wrapped around my skin that you were mine. I knew when I looked into your blue eyes that I loved you.

Now I have spoken to you, Stan. You have heard my voice. You have judged my voice, you have judged me. I tape my own voice to hear what I sounded like to you. To hear what you heard when you spoke to me. But I replay these tapes and I cannot really hear anything. I just sound like a crying voice. I cannot judge my voice like you can. I cannot judge my nose or my chin like you can either. Only you can judge me and I don't know the criteria. I don't know. I will listen to the tapes over and over again until I decide what I have to do. Once I figure out what my voice sounds like to you I will know what to do next.

I have decided I will not turn into a pervert like my crazy uncle, uncle number one. The one who is still alive, but is a pervert, I will not turn into an animal like him. I can still see him pacing around repeating, Nobody sits with me anymore. Nobody sits with me anymore. Then he would go in his room and write about how nobody sits with him anymore. He would stain paper with words about how nobody sits with him anymore. I knew I would be like this someday. This is why I started making myself orgasm at a very young age, so that I would never be a pervert. I remember saying to myself, nobody will ever touch you. Nobody can ever want to touch you. You have to learn to make yourself happy, little girl. All those girls who call you Humper will have boys to touch them when they grow up, so they don't have to touch themselves, but you do, or you will go crazy. I am older now. I never got to be kissed by a young boy because when I was young no young boy wanted to kiss me. I know young boys kiss differently than old men. I just don't know how. I know lips are new things to a boy who is young. My crazy uncle wanted me when I was young at least. Because he wanted everything, or anything. Yes, he is an animal, but he wanted to touch me. The lonely, perverted, garbage collecting animal wanted me. I remember one day he woke me up by tenderly stroking my cheeks. I opened my eyes and saw his gnarled, smiling face above me. Only this man knows that my young face was as soft as a rose petal.

What do I have to do to be like Leam Osheay? I have to be strong. I have to be good and brave. I have to be gorgeous. I have to drive really fast without being scared. I have to paint fucking. I have to beat men up who try to touch me in bars. I have to speak many languages. I have to not want men. I can't do it, Stan. I can't be Leam Osheay. This makes me want to howl and yelp with humiliation. No, I will pace around and around to music instead. I will not cry. I will get up and turn on some music and pace in front of the window in my room.

I saw my cousin with him. Yes, my cousin Kindness. She took me with her when she met up with a friend of a friend. I was maybe four, or five, or six, or seven. It was maybe summer, spring, fall, or winter. She held my hand as we walked behind him up the stairs of the motel. Then, when we got to the room she put me in the bathroom and locked the door. I could hear them laughing and talking, and then moaning. I said, nicely at first, please let me out. Then I started screaming. I banged on the door until they got upset. Hanan finally came over and opened the door with a blanket wrapped around her shoulders. They let me out and they let me watch. He was on top of her and she had no underwear on. I know she didn't because I saw her underwear on the floor. He was moving on top of her. She was making sounds. He was putting his tongue in her face. I got so sad. I said Hanan loves me. Hanan is going to do with me whatever she is doing with you when we get home. They laughed. I screamed. I can do it too! I can do what you are doing. He lifted the covers and said, come on then. Come on, Baby. Come over here. I will show you how to do it. But I couldn't move. I was sad and I didn't want to do it with him. I wanted to do it with Hanan. I was so sad. It was as if I had never seen so much skin. There was so much oddly shaped skin on him. I said I don't want to do it right now, but I will do it later with Hanan. My best friend says that I really just didn't want to believe Hanan loved him more than she loved me. I wanted to believe Hanan loved me, and only me, because she was my best friend at the time. So I did it. I did what the boy did with Hanan. We went back to her room and I got on top of Hanan and moved around. I was Hanan, and Hanan was the boy. I told her she had to kiss me too, like the boy kissed her, because she was the boy. She kissed me. I said, no, you have to kiss me like you kissed him. Hanan said she would if I didn't tell anybody what I saw. I promised I would never tell anybody. I swore to God. But Hanan stuck her tongue in my mouth and I still told my father what I saw. She let me move my lips up and down her mouth while I wiggled my little cunt around her hips and I still told. I touched her everywhere he did, then I told. It was just too strange what they were doing. It just looked so strange. It felt so strange doing it too. But I knew that's what made the boy special to Hanan. I want to be special to Hanan too. I want to be special to women I love. I told my father because I knew he would think it was strange. He did. I made him swear to never tell Hanan that I told him. My father made me take off my underwear and he told Hanan that I told him anyway. He made me take off my underwear, then he told. He yelled at Hanan in front of me. He said it was a bad thing she did. I kept my head down so she couldn't stare at me. He wouldn't have known what she had done unless I had shown him. I should not have taken off my underwear. I obviously did not love Hanan. I took my underwear off. Then a few minutes later he said, put your underwear back on. Take your underwear off. Put your underwear back on. What does a father do with his child in the meantime? He keeps his arms around her shoulders and stares up at the ceiling with her. He loves her. He wants her to be happy. So, with her underwear off, he tells her the meaning of life.

This is what it would be like if Leam and Stan ever made love: he would kiss her face, and she would kiss his face, and they would take each other's clothes off, then he would kiss her body, and she would kiss his body. It sounds just like fucking, but it would be love making because when Leam and Stan do it then you need two words for it. People do the same things every time they make love. There is the kissing of the nipples and then the insertion of something somewhere, or the insertion of something somewhere then the kissing of the nipples. However, nipples are usually kissed, or sucked, or nibbled on at some point. Stan would know how to touch Leam's breasts. He would know that if he wants her to get excited about him getting excited then he should use firm pressure, but if he wants her to be excited because her body wants him then he should be very, very slow and soft. The lightest touch goes a long way with Leam. Leam likes lovemaking to feel like it did when she accidentally came too close to a rose bush and the rose petals brushed up against her breasts. She turned and looked at the red roses. She wanted so much to open her mouth wide and stuff her throat with them. She wanted to stand with her legs far apart and stuff herself with red roses. She didn't though because Leam is beautiful. Leam is too beautiful to ever do anything bad. I know all about what light touch can do to Leam because my brother and I have tickled our mother with the tips of our fingers before. We were just joking with her. We were very short so our faces came up to her ass, so that is where we tickled her. We moved our fingers around in circles lightly and she squirmed. She said, stop it. Stop it! You don't know how that makes me feel. I didn't know how it made her feel, but I knew even then that when you touch people slowly and softly it makes people feel something. I knew this from watching Hanan with the boy. My mom said she was upset with us. But she was probably just upset because no man had ever made her feel that way. My mother is meant for a nice guy, too, but she doesn't have one. I get on pillows and I think about the part they took away from her. I get on pillows in honor of my mother, because they did not cut that part out of me in the desert. Humper was born in the desert too.

Humper couldn't take off her shoes once. She was in a locker room during gym class and she tried to take off her pants with her shoes still on. Humper was wearing large, cheap shoes. The pants wouldn't come all the way off and then the shoes wouldn't come off because they were covered by pants. Humper was stuck. Humper asked the only person in the locker room who didn't care that boy number one thought Humper looked like a dog to help her pull her pants off. This person did try to help but she couldn't pull Humper's pants off. The other people in the locker room did care that boy number one thought Humper looked like a dog. They thought it was so funny. Humper was sitting there on that bench with her underwear still on, asking somebody to pull off her pants because she couldn't get her pants or her shoes off. They mimicked Humper's movements. They mimicked Humper's voice. And they laughed and laughed. Help me. Pull, Humper kept saying. Help me, pull, they screamed and laughed. Pull! Pull! Humper went home after school every night. She went to the room every night and pretended a boy was touching her. She pretended a boy was on top of her, then she pretended that she was on top of the boy. The first time she did this she explained to God silently that she was only sinning because she had to, because nobody else would ever touch her. The other children didn't have to sin because somebody would touch them someday. The first time Humper orgasmed she realized why men fight over women in films. She knew why women do not always leave men who say mean things to them. The first time she orgasmed she was in the tub and water from the showerhead was coming down on her head. Sometimes Humper would take her pillow into the bathroom with her when nobody was looking. On the bathroom floor she would get on top of the pillow with her face burning and her eyes swollen and pretend the pillow was Hanan, and that Hanan was a man. She would say to the pillow silently, make me feel happy pillow, Sir. Only you will ever make me feel good, because only you can. The pillow would stare back, obviously willing, but dead and sad. The pillow was an innocent, a baby animal. The pillow would make Humper orgasm over and over again, but then Humper would cry. After she cried she would try to cut her right hand off so she could still go to heaven someday. If the sinning body part offends you then cast it into the fire, God said something like that. Humper held a knife up above her wrist in the room at night. She did this after she orgasmed, when nobody was watching. Humper would always move the knife over, above her fingers. A little finger is easier to discard than a whole hand is. Still she could not do it. She did not want to go to heaven and be happy. She chose her right hand. She chose her right index finger over God. That is why no matter what she does now she will not have Stan. Stan will be with Leam. Her big brown eyes next to his green eyes are lovely in the wedding pictures.

Can I have a long island iced tea please?

Would you please make me a long island iced tea?

I would love a long island iced tea.

I will have a long island iced tea.

Who gives this woman to this man?

Who gives this man to this woman?

God says I do. I do. I give Stan to Leam and I give Leam to Stan, because she is not a pillow humping animal.

I will have a long island iced tea. Thanks.

Thank you.

Stan, let's stop and look at that woman in the wheel-chair outside our window. Would you want her? Do you want her, Stan? Could you want her, Stan? Does she orgasm? Has a man who she has wanted to make love to ever wanted to make love back to her? And all those women on the earth holding their starving babies with flies on their faces, do you want them too? I would imagine that women with starving babies are prone to having many orgasms. I imagine that most of the men who would want to make love to them more than once are not awkward. What does it look like on a woman, waking up in the morning after having been made love to? Can you see it on their faces in the morning, a gentle glow, a happiness? Is that what I look like after I have been with my pillow all night? Can everybody on the train see it on me? If I could have just made love to Stan the way Leam does then we would be together. If I could just be wild in bed then my life would be much better. My life could have a meaning. I could be normal. Then I could go on to starve if I wanted to and I would still be happy.

What is wrong with me that only the awkward friend of a friend would want to fuck me more than once? What is wrong with me? What am I? So, I ask my uncle why this is happening to me. He is with God in heaven now, so he knows things that I don't know. I need advice. I need a father to tell me that I am good and that Stan is bad. So I ask him, Uncle, why doesn't anybody want to make love to me? And he says some men do want to make love to you, but not the ones you want to make love to you. I ask him, why can't the ones I want be the ones who want me? He says because you have been fucked too many times, now only the men who would make love to anything, or everything, would want to make love to you, like my crazy perverted brother. Oh, and God says to tell you that nobody will make love to a woman who has been fucked so often by a pillow. Now you are sad. No, I am not. Yes, you are. Do you remember when you were a little girl and you said that if God says that he is love, and he also says that he is the way, then really love is the way. You compared it to an algebraic equation: God equals love, God equals the way, love equals the way. I had to tell you that God is not like algebra. Yes, I remember. I was really happy when I thought I had figured out the meaning of life. I was happy that all you have to do is love people and then you go to heaven, but you told me that God is not like algebra. Well, that is what you are. You have been fucked by your pillow and you think about stabbing people in the ear. You are an animal. You want to be miserable. You don't want to be happy. No man will love you unless you are completely happy before you even meet him. But you refused to choose happiness over your finger. People feel how miserable you are and misery is not what they want for themselves. They know they will only live once. It is really very simple, but you still don't understand it. You know why you started touching yourself at such a young age? Because you knew, and you know, that nobody would ever want to make love to you like they want to make love to Leam. You knew you had to touch yourself, but now

you are crying about it like a crazy animal. Your father wouldn't even make love to you. He just wanted
you to take your underwear off. That is why that is all
you can remember. That is all that happened. Do you
remember having to put your underwear back on after
the few minutes that you don't remember? Well, I am
in heaven now, so I can tell you that nothing happened.
He held you in his arms and you both stared at the
ceiling with your underwear off. You just wish somebody had wanted to touch you then because nobody
wants to touch you now. No, I wish something bad had
happened to me so I would have a right to feel sad. Do
you remember him telling you to put your underwear
back on? Yes, you are a crazy animal. Why don't you
know how to be a good person? Leam knows how to
be a good person. But I don't know how, Uncle. That
is why I am speaking to you. You tell me how to be a
good person. You are with God now, you know these
things. You said you know all about these things. You
are the one who knew that God is not like algebra. Ask
God what I should do and then tell me what I should
do. God doesn't know what you should do. He made
you too hairy. You are not special. Nobody wants to
make love to you, because you are not very special. I
can hear my uncle laughing. I am happy. He thinks I
am funny, not nice and awkward. This is why I will
now bend down and apologize to him as he is dying.
Forgive me, I say silently, I should have been kinder to

you so you could eventually intercede on my behalf. I should have just been kinder to you. You will always be the closest I have come to having a father. But you do not love me because when I was eight in the summer I wouldn't let you buy me ice cream. It was really just my pride, but I told myself that I was only trying to be kind. You don't love me because when I was eight in the winter I wouldn't let you give me a ride to school. I thought it was good to not take things from people. I thought it was kind. You don't love me because when I was fourteen in the fall you hugged me and I made a face. I was happy that you hugged me on my birthday, I am just awkward sometimes. But this made you feel awkward, and nobody loves an awkward person who makes them feel awkward too.

All right.

It is all right.

All right, now think of something happy. Men with bent backs. Ugly men. Men holding their hats in their hands, waiting in line to fuck me. The stronger, harder bodies of balmy, shivering men.

I do sometimes wonder how often people wash down there and how well. I know I wash well only because I often think about not being clean down there, but I really don't need to worry about it since nobody gets close enough to smell those parts of me. Sometimes I meet a boy though and I think I would do this and that to you if you want, but I don't know how well you wash down there. I am probably just concerned with smelling clean because that is the one thing I can do to be happy. Yes, that must be it. I will really try to figure everything else out right now. I will figure everything out. My problem is not that I am unhappy, I am just not sincere enough. I do not feel enough. I need to be more honest with myself and others. I will get to know myself and figure everything out right now.

Right now.

My cunt is a man on a bus hugging a bag of groceries. It wants to be warm. It wants life to be bright like cartoons are. It wants groceries to be there when it is hungry and a thick, soft, colorful bed to sleep on at night. That will make my cunt feel safe, because it is an animal, but it is people too. It walks to the cupboards at night, waits with anticipation to open them, knowing there will be bread there. It stands over the sink and quickly eats the bread in its hand. It opens the refrigerator to make sure all the packages are still arranged in rows. Then it walks back to its bed, holds on to its pillow, and falls asleep. My cunt is a man who has been stabbed in the ear. It has been harmed, but has escaped attention.

All of its water has left it and nobody watches. My cunt is a nice guy. It does awkward things but it cannot hurt me. I do not want it, but it would have me. My cunt is a dying uncle. I can apologize to it, but it may still stay angry. My cunt is a crazy uncle. It is a lonely pervert who collects garbage. It will sloppily take me against my will if I let it. My cunt is a good man too, and we belong to each other. No, it is not where urine leaves my body. It is where blood leaves my body. There are so many different parts to this one part of me that I do not bother to use all the different names for them. I want only one word. Men come in and blood goes out. It is all covered by thick, coarse hair, but it is made of very tender, soft skin. When you open it up you see skin the color of blood when it is inside my body. When you look closer you find out there is a tunnel there that is the color of blood when it is outside of my body. On the left side of my cunt a flag-like patch of wrinkled, tender, soft skin dangles down. It wanted to keep dangling down further and further but it is attached to my body. It is the reason I cannot balance. I do not make sense. It is the reason they cut at my mother. Now my mother can walk without her excess skin dangling down in between her thighs and rubbing against her. Now my mother can live without wanting to touch herself. The part of me that wanted to be tucked away, folded in skin that is covered by hair, and the part of me that wanted to see what there was to see outside my body are both here. There are many other parts of me that are my cunt. They are all either pulpy purple, blue, or red. I will let you touch it, because I want to be honest with you, because I want to be sincere. Stan, you cannot stare at it.

The complete list of humiliation is as follows: a boy, when I was twenty-three in the summer; when I was twenty-four in the fall; when I was twenty-four in the winter; when I was twenty-five in the spring; when I was twenty-six in the fall; when I was twenty-six in the fall; when I was twenty-six in the fall; when I was twenty-six in the fall; when I was twenty-seven in the winter; when I was twenty-seven in the winter; when I was twenty-seven in the winter; when I was twenty-seven in the winter; when I was twenty-eight in the winter; when I was thirty in the spring. I need an age and a season because that is all I know happened. That is all I know happened to me. It is, maybe, what I am. I need seasons because being fucked by a man who does not want me, every so often, is like a drop of water falling, every so often, on an empty frying pan that has been left on a flame for years and years. If you don't try to remember when it fell, the drop just disappears. Then you can't be happy because you feel that nobody loves you and nobody ever wants to touch you. It is only because you don't remember. I will pace and try to remember, and I will make a list of humiliation in my head. Once I remember everything I will write them all down and put the list above my bed. Then I will know myself and be happy.

On his final day my uncle was grunting. His mouth was open too wide, bloody sores encrusted around his lips. His tongue was twitching inside his mouth. His eyes, open too wide and yellow with bile, embedded inside his face. His abdomen seemingly contorted, looked like a piece of art, wrapped with bandages. And he was grunting. He was reaching for something with his mouth. His body would not follow his mouth. His body was keeping him somewhere where his mouth did not want to be. I see him now. He is reaching towards heaven with his mouth. Go there and pray for me, Uncle. You are the only father I have ever really had. I am sorry we could not be kinder to each other. And what do the kamikaze swallows of the world think of this? It is all just biology, biology, biology. But I know everything happens for a reason. Uncles die so you can pray to them eventually and get what you want from God. I want Stan. I leaned in close and apologized to him before he died. I whispered in his ears. I am sorry for all the things that happened to me, and to you, and to you and me because of each other. It could have been a very tender moment, but I quickly realized that I had only apologized in hopes that he would apologize back. I started crying then. Because my uncle was just art now. Because it was a tender moment to share with the dying, that could only be tender if the dying would give you what you had always wanted from them before they died. It was getting too complicated when it was supposed to be only simple and tender.

My family is slowly shrinking, but my mother is still alive. I want to wash every inch of my mother's body before she dies. I want to study her. You see, my mother and I are identical from the neck down. I want to see what else will go wrong with my body, what will happen to me, and what I am. I already know that my nose moves when I speak too. I know why the veins on my hands are so prominent. We have hair in exactly the same places. I assume my breath also leaves its mark. All of my body, all of my body is a copy of my mother. She gave me her breasts, which you think are my best feature. But still if I could have chosen before I was born I would not have picked my mother's body. She is short with black hair and brown eyes. He skin color is similar to the color of a long island iced tea. My mother and I would make animals speak to each other when I was a child. We would have the plastic giraffes marry the plastic lions. The animals would meet while we were sitting on the floor. Then they would marry when we marched them around the bed and sang. I should have known then that we are the same. My feet will also smell like this, I should have thought while the elephant was asking the bear if he would take his zebra bride to have and to hold forever and ever. We called it playing weddings. It was our favorite thing to do together. I should have known. My crazy uncle always wanted a wedding, but he can't get married because he is crazy and ugly. Nobody could ever want him. When he was a child he lost his hearing. Nobody could talk to him so he slowly became more and more lonely. He became more and more crazy. And as he became more and more crazy he collected more and more garbage in our backyard. I know all about the people on the trains because of my crazy uncle. I know how people could let millions of other people get on trains right before their very eyes. My crazy uncle always wanted to keep the babies of the stray cats that lived around our house. He would take them from their mother and keep them in a box and put the box in a shed where he keeps his garbage. The first thing I do, of course, is try to explain that baby cats need their mother so they can live. But that does not work. My uncle thinks he loves the baby cats because he thinks baby cats can love him back. He thinks they will make him happy because they will not go away. So, I try to secretly give them back to their mother, but the mother does not go very far because my crazy uncle is feeding her. The baby cats end up in a box again. I can hear them crying at night. Baby cats trapped in a box without their mother cry constantly. They must feel humiliated. I want to help them, I think to myself. After a few minutes of that I begin to think, I feel sad for you baby cats. I imagine what it would feel like to be alone and hungry in a box in a shed full of garbage without a mother. Then I start thinking, I am sorry this is happening to you baby cats, but what can I do? Then I finally make myself believe that there is nothing I can do. So, I have to learn to just hear them cry without listening to them crying. Otherwise I will still feel sad for the baby cats even though there is nothing I can do. Then I start wishing they could just stop crying already so I don't have to work so hard at pretending not to listen to them while lying in bed. Then I wish they could die, so they could stop crying, and I wouldn't have to hear them and I wouldn't have to pretend. They would be better off if they just died. They are unhappy and pitiful. Then I just stop hearing them cry altogether. Yes, I don't even have to struggle with thinking anything to myself anymore. The baby cats cry, I don't hear them, and when I do, accidentally, I think about how stupid they are to have let themselves be put in a situation like this. They have put themselves in this position where they are trapped in a box in a shed without milk from their mother. Stupid stray cats, there must be something wrong with them. You deserve this. What did you do to end up in a box? If you were better your mother would have loved you. Now, you can only cry like stupid animals just waiting to die. But the baby cats are sad and they may not even know it. I am sad too because I can't really feel being fucked, so I have to have ways to work around it. When I was with the old man I would ask him how it feels to be inside me. I would ask him this because I felt nothing when he was inside me. He would say, My cock feels like it's going to explode. He never wondered why I could ask so calmly. If I felt at all like exploding myself, then how could I have asked so calmly? What does it feel like, old man? My cock feels like it's going to explode. Well, that's good, I suppose.

The baby cats and the bird that came to the window sill are bad. Why would a bird come to my window sill? Is it sad, is it sick? If it is broken, then I don't want it on my window sill. It is only a beautiful bird if it can fly, be happy without me. Why didn't you save the worm that you knew would die outside of the dirt? Because it will die anyway. All you had to do it was put it back in the dirt. Why didn't I save the people on the trains? Why doesn't he have to love me if only to be kind to me? If only because it hurts me so much that he doesn't love me? Because you will die anyway. And he will die anyway. Because the bird was not beautiful until it flew away, until you saw how it could live without you, until I realized it was only at my window sill for a few minutes. That is the difference between pigeons and doves. There is a difference between ladybugs and potato bugs. The name says it all. When a beautiful butterfly is young, it is a pretty caterpillar. When an ugly fly is young, it is an ugly maggot. If you look different, then you are different, and that is all there is to it. But even the ugly spiders flee so they can live. An ugly octopus will climb up arms to escape the heat coming from a pot. Its nerve endings tell it there is danger. It wants to live even though people think it is ugly. Because it does not know it will not live long anyway. It wants to live because it knows it does not have very long to live. I must want to live because I am not dying. I will not die. But I will not live just because God wants me to. I am a cockroach like they said. Cockroaches are made of water too. We are both made mostly of water. Eight-and-a-half parts out of ten of our brain is water. Eight parts of our blood is water. Seven parts of our muscle is water. We are water that sits and stands still. We move and speak and still mean nothing. Give life and take life like water, like God, but still are clear like water, like God. Yes, I have figured it all out. Only things that are made of water can die. The other things, like rocks and dirt, are only eroded, changed by water. Things that are made of water have nerve endings. Nerve endings are the reason these things feel pain. Yes, things made of water feel pain, though water itself does not. If I had seen Christ walk on water I would not have thought it was a miracle, said a boy. I would just have wondered how Christ taught himself to walk on water. The boy said this to let me know that he is special. The boy will not believe in God no matter what happens to the boy.

If there is a God then you made sure purposely that there were nerve endings on our lips. You would have something to do with the fact that four thousand nerve endings are on the tip of the boy's cock and eight thousand nerve endings on the tip of the girl's cunt. Eight thousand nerve endings on an organ that is very difficult to find. Four thousand nerve endings in a place that's very easy to find. Why God? Why did you do this? Because I want you to have a way of finding out if he loves you, but I want him to always believe he is loved. That way you can know if a man loves you. If he can find all those nerve endings, then you know you are loved. At least you will feel loved. They cut them out of my mother, God, now she is lonely. But now you can know he doesn't love you and he will always think he is loved. His cock is going to explode. Thank you, God.

I am trying to figure everything out with you right now. What can I keep and what can you take away? What can you keep forever and ever and ever? Yes, what is mine? Well, you can lose your job. This means that you can lose your money. Losing your money means that you can lose bread and the room. Losing bread and the room means that you will be hungry and cold. You can lose people that you love. They can leave you or they can die. Hopefully they die but don't leave you because people leaving you means something about who you are, but people dying means something about me, God. You can lose so much that even your dream of being an old lady, in an old room, on an old bed and only having sleep to comfort you at night cannot come true. Let's see, what can you keep? You can keep your skin. I have never heard of somebody being skinned alive and living for too long after that. If you are living you must have some skin. Burned skin, or scarred skin, or dead skin, maybe, but it is still skin. All right, what will I have if I can only be sure that I will have a life with skin? You will have wind. You will be able to feel the wind with your skin. Can I have Stan's lips on my back? I will have Stan's fingertips making baby circles on my back. I will have Stan's hands on the skin of my face. I can lose everything and still have Stan. Thank you. Thank you for helping me figure everything out.

What do you think Stan would be if he were a dessert? Cake is a dessert. Desserts are things you eat when you are full. You eat them only to taste them. You do not eat desserts because you are hungry. You do not need a dessert. You have to be happy without desserts. That is what people tell me about having Stan. They say I have to be happy without him so I can have him. But wouldn't the dessert enjoy being eaten first? Wouldn't the dessert like knowing that you didn't wait until you were full, happy, before you wanted him? Wouldn't the dessert appreciate being needed just like real bread is? Stan would be a perfect dessert, one that fills you up, not too sweet, but sweet enough. You can have him for breakfast and you can have him after dinner.

What could have happened is that my father could have said, Show me, how did she take off her underwear? I showed him and then he said, I am going to touch your body. I am going to touch all the places where there will someday be hair. I will slowly run my hands down your arms and your stomach and all the other places where you are soft and tender now because you will not be soft or tender later when the hair comes. My father knew then that hair ruins everything. No matter what you do to get rid of it, it comes back. It can even grow right under the skin and leave ugly bumps on the skin. It makes the skin ugly. Or what could have happened is that my father could have said, Show me, how did she take off her underwear? I showed him and then he thought, Kindness, you little whore. You took my innocent child to watch you take your underwear off. I know you did this to Hanan because she just showed me. She is young, but she can mimic what she sees. That is precisely why I asked her to show me. That is the only reason. It took him a while to think all these things. After he thought about all this for a while he said, Put your underwear back on. My father is a baby. He does not know how to be kind, he does not know how to be mean, he does not really know anything. He is only a baby who nobody loves. By the time I was born he had chosen not to love anybody, since nobody had ever really loved him.

List of My Father's Humiliations: number one, when he was born and the two brothers he was born with died; number two, every time he did something bad his mother said that he was possessed by the spirits of his two brothers; number three, every time he touched his mother and she thought about his two dead brothers; number four, when he pushed his father down the stairs; number five, every time his sister, Hanan's mother, said something mean to him about my mother.

If you are God then some things you think of don't make any sense. For example, why do bees die once they sting you if why they sting you is because they don't want to die? Why would you fool bees like that? Why do you make a fool out of bees? To teach them a lesson. To let them know, in My own hard way, that they need to be happy if they are to ever find love. To teach them how to be good bees so they don't go to hell. It is My way of saying, don't be scared little bees, even though you can lose everything. Don't feel fear and loneliness or you will sting somebody and then you will die and be alone forever.

All right then. If you are really God then tell me about hell. Hell is being shot out into space. Hell is staying alive without gravity in darkness. Hell is realizing that those pretty rings around planets are actually made out of huge moving rocks. Hell is feeling the heat and being stung by the sulfur. Recognizing, finally, how difficult and complicated it must have been for me to make stars for you. Hell is knowing that you should have been more grateful for those pretty little lights that come out at night. All this while it is too late. You were wrong to be so sad, to want arms so much, to think I am mean for letting the people put the people on trains. The fear of hell is why earth cannot leave the sun. Then I am not scared to go to hell because in this meat I am safe. The sulfur would choke me instantly. The heat would disintegrate me immediately. I would fall only briefly until rock slams into my face. I would not be able to experience this hell and stay alive to experience it. God, you are merciful that way. Yes, I am. Instead I put the sulfur in your mouth. I put the sinking feeling in your stomach. You walk around with this list of humiliation in your chest. You feel as if you are always falling. This makes you feel heavy and weightless at the same time, as if there is no gravity. You do not die, you feel this and live. You must want to die though, but you can't, so you don't. Thank you, God.

I want my best friend to come into my room right now. I want her to hold me. I want her to tell me that she loves me. I want her to say she is sorry for apologizing so coldly and take me in her arms. I am sorry I always apologize with such brevity. It's all right. I love you. I always have loved you. Well, I have always been sorry about the brevity and coldness with which I apologized, I just couldn't tell you. I know. I know you never wanted me to wait in the room alone. I got on a train to go see you and I had to listen to you make love to your boyfriend. I sat on a train for three days to visit you because you were stressed. You never would have me cry in the room alone. You are my best friend and we love each other. Just because I cannot orgasm like you can does not mean we cannot know each other for the rest of our lives. If I did not know you, and you did not hold me at night, my thoughts would be wasted like my body. If they are all your men, then you must be my one woman.

I sit in a corner of the room alone. I have a pen and I have a naked doll. I take the pen and try to stick it all the way in the little hole on the button at the bottom of the doll. It will not go in, I have to keep pushing and pushing. I push despite how the doll resists and how much the pen resists. Does it feel good? No, it hurts, the doll says. It hurts but it feels good too, you mean?

98

I don't know. I don't remember. It does not really hurt and it does not really feel good, it feels like there is always a finger inside me. That's good. You know what you are now.

Bread is wasted when it is thrown away. Water is wasted when nobody who wants to live gets to drink it. What makes a body wasted? When nobody appreciates it? If nobody can recognize your ears in a line up, then you might as well have never had ears at all, my best friend says. If nobody thinks your legs are beautiful then they never existed, or at least they were never beautiful. My best friend loved the boy she had made love to so loudly because he was not like the boy before him who said mean things about her legs. The bad man would ask her if she thinks it is all right for him to walk around with a girlfriend whose legs look like that. It was a rhetorical question. He wanted her to say I don't deserve you. You don't deserve these legs. I love my best friend's legs. But that is not what matters to her. A man must love legs for them to be really loved. I know this too. My best friend wants to find a man who will love life so much that she can feel it, so that life can be loved. I want to find a man who will want to touch me so much that I can finally feel it, so that I can be loved. We both should just get what we need from each other and forget about the boys. Yin and yin makes stronger, better yin, and yin is what we already are. But when boy number fourteen kissed me and then did not want to kiss me again I could not forget about him. He kissed me the way I wanted to be kissed. The way my pillow kisses me, the way I would kiss myself, the way I do kiss myself. That is why he could have been my man. The beautiful kiss turned into a discarded little baby's finger. A little baby's finger that was beautiful, when it was attached to its baby. Cut off of the baby's hand it became carnage, little baby carnage. Our bodies know how to consume, take and discard. Why don't you and I know how to consume, take and discard? The memory of that beautiful kiss, once I realized it had been with a man who did not want to kiss me again, turned into a beautiful immovable finger, attached but useless.

Right now on the earth there is one person dying for every person being born. Right now most people on the planet are hungry because they do not have enough bread. Right now on this earth very few people can eat. And what I want is you, Stan. And the earth does not even know it is spinning. It spins around itself so many times that it makes a trip around the entire sun. Then it does it again and again, over and over. One out of three of the people on the earth are fair skinned. One out of three of the people on the earth believe in Christ. Another one out of three of the people on the earth do not. More than one out of two of the people on the earth live in only one part of the earth. But this is what

Stan looks like on the inside, he is cake. He is cake that is not too sweet, but really rich still. He is cake you can have for breakfast, but also save for dessert.

If you are God then did you make people only so you can hear songs? Was it Your own hard way of turning the music on? Do you make us miserable so we can sing sad songs? Do you make us miserable so when something good happens we can be happy enough to sing happy songs? If you already know everything then did you just want to watch us wonder what is wrong? Is this funny to you? Me, pacing here, the music is playing and I can't even hear it. What are you thinking as I pace around to music I can't hear? What do you think about all the people whose hands get chopped off by other people?

If a tree falls in the middle of a forest, but nobody hears it, then was it really a tree? If you go around breathing and being what you are, but nobody in the world really knows you well enough to know what you are, then are you really who you are? Are you anything at all? If nobody touches your body then do you have a body?

I want to make music with my body for you, God. I want to scratch at my feet to make music. I want to pick at my skin to make music. I want to shred my hair and make music. I want to slap my face and file my teeth to make music for you. If there is a heaven then it is where I can slap my own face to make beautiful music for God. Bang my head on a wall until God claps his hands.

Is being raped at all like being made to swallow your own vomit? Is that why we kill each other? Yes. Is that why we kill ourselves? But even if you are raped you will get over it. Yes, you will. Time does heal all wounds. Yes, it does. I made you that way. The amount of memory storage capacity in your brain is finite. Your brain, which is mostly water, is finite. New memories push the other memories back. The new memories of waking up push the older memories of waking up out of the way. The more new memories are made, the more the old ones have to become weaker and weaker, smaller and smaller, to make space. You will all forget. So we do not ever have to forgive, but we have to forget eventually so the memory of where the keys are today can fit in our brains. That's why if you don't forget then you will go crazy, too many memories. You won't be able to remember whether or not you did the things you had to do that day. I cannot forget. Then you will lose your job and be cold and hungry. All because somebody left you or somebody died.

One of my mother's friends died like my uncle. She used to tell me the story about a girl and the flowers that made her beautiful every time she came to visit us. The girl was ugly until she gave the thirsty flowers water, even though she knew the mean witch she lived with would hurt her if she came back without any water. The sunflower made her tall and thin. The rose made her lips a pretty shade of red. The jasmine made her skin as milky as jasmine petals. I would beg her to tell me the story again and again. Every time she came to visit I would ask her to tell me the story again and she would agree to do so. She told it so well, every single time, exactly the same way. Her face would change the same way, every time making the same expressions. Her voice would change the same way, every time rising and falling on the same words. There was once a girl who lived with a mean hairy witch. The witch was so mean that the girl was always scared of her. The witch would always make her do all the chores around the house because all she wanted to do all day was comb her hairy body. She would always ask the girl to comb her hairy body for her. The girl would have to comb the witch for hours everyday. One day the witch told the girl to go get her some water. The girl took the bucket and went off to the well. This time on her way back to the witch's house she noticed that the sunflower was moving its head toward her. She was so startled. The sunflower lowered its head and said I am so thirsty won't you please give me some water. But the witch will be so angry with me if I don't come back with a full bucket of water, the girl said. But I am so thirsty, won't you please give me some water. All right, I will give you my water. The sunflower was so grateful it cried, thanked the girl. And suddenly she grew taller. My mother's friend had never been married. There must have been something wrong with her body that made her impossible to make love to. But I was young, I couldn't see it. So there we were, the young and the old girl, wishing we were beautiful. The young girl, the old girl, and the fairy tale from the desert, where water is scarce. We both knew why we were alone. We would not have given those flowers the water they wanted because we would have been too scared of the mean witch. We did not give water to the people on the trains. We were too weak on the inside to ever be beautiful on the outside, even if we wanted to be. We should have posed for a portrait together, but we did not. We should have held each other and smiled at the painter because we were so happy to know what we are.

Do you really want to be happy though? Yes, God, I do. What happens once you are happy? Happiness, happiness, happiness is the great big hole. Maybe you want to simply want to be happy. Maybe you want to want to want to be happy. Want, after all, is a feeling you can have to hold, and to love, and keep forever. Happiness is only a feeling for a day or two until you get used to it. You mean if I ever had Stan in my arms then there would be nothing else to want? Then I would have to feel something for the starving babies and their women and all the people who have been murdered and raped. Even if they had a Stan too, I would have a Stan and bread and the room, so I would have to be nice. That is just too much good for one person to have. You are right, I would have to feel happy all the time and that is too hard. I cannot do that. To have to laugh at stupid jokes and paint pretty pictures all the time is just too hard.

I cannot live without knowing the meaning of life. So I will figure it out right now. First, we are born and we have bodies. We are told we will die and are given different reasons for that. We are told about God. But we still have to work so we can have bread and a room. We lose the bread and the room and our bodies hurt. We cannot think or feel much when our bodies hurt. When our bodies hurt we can only feel our bodies. It is good if your body does not hurt so you can be free to love. If you have food and shelter and you love people then you are happy. Why are we ever happy if we are all meat that rots in dirt? Well, because before that happens then you get to be good and maybe you will go to heaven. What if there is no heaven? Then you just live to be happy right now. Why does happiness matter if you were nothing, then you are something, then you become dirt. Because maybe there is something you are doing right now that can make you happy.

One alien says if all the good ones are in heaven that means there are zillions of them in heaven. By the time we get to attack then it will be zillions and zillions of them. The other one says, but do most of them go to heaven, aren't most of them bad? Yes, but even if only some of them go to heaven then that is still zillions of them. Heaven must be a big place, bigger than the universe. Yes, it must be. Why do they think anything matters to them again? Why do some of them care about the people on the trains? We think it is because they think they can change the earth. But even if they did change something right now it would only be for a few minutes, it would change only so it could change back. They must have noticed how everybody goes back to killing once they stop the killing. Yes, once they stop themselves from killing each other in one place they begin killing each other in another place. They are in a predicament. They live, then they die, and they don't really know why, or what happens afterwards. How sad. Yes, how sad. That's it. This must be why they get so upset.

When the aliens come to get us I will be in a large building made of marble and stone. It will be dark blue and breezy indoors because of what the aliens have done to the weather. My skin will prickle and I will want to be tamped down. Everybody else will be running around in their suits and dresses. I will walk slowly past them all to try and find the aliens. I will make a turn into a stone hallway. I see one of them. We are all alone. He has gray skin and wisps of bright brown hair. He is much larger than I am, but I know somehow that he is just a baby. He is one of their children. He has only two eyes but five mouths. The mouths are on top and next to each other with the largest mouth in the middle, with two short tongues in each mouth. He comes closer to me. He does not love me, but he wants to know what I am. He does not know I am not beautiful. He is young, he cannot see it. He bends to lower me to the ground softly. He puts his mouths on my face. He is kissing me, but only to know me. There are tongues on my mouth and my nose and my chin and my cheeks. I want him to move his head down but he doesn't, that is not how alien babies make love. I want what he is doing to make me orgasm, but it will not. I cannot do anything now but lie there underneath him and pretend to love him. This makes me cry. This makes him want to shut me up. He begins to whisper in my ear. Baby, don't you worry your pretty little head about it he says. He has obviously already learned something about being a human man from touching a woman's face. He tells me what he thinks about the beauty of human blood, the rarity of its shade of red among all the shades of red in the universe. How they travel all over the universe just to see it. How when people make other people line up so they can shoot many people all at once their blood gushes quickly as their bodies shudder, turning people into beautiful, bright, dancing fountains. He says this is not sad, it is beautiful. Thank you. That's all I needed to know. People kill people because blood is beautiful. I came and came beneath him.

I am tired of that joke people make. You know, the one about how little boys think it is disgusting to be kissed by beautiful women when they are little boys, but when they grow up they will want to be kissed by beautiful women. You've heard the joke before. Yes, you have. I know you have. It usually comes up when a group of people are together and a woman kisses a little boy and the little boy says something like, yuck, or tries to get away from the woman. Then one of the adults says something like, just wait until you are older, you'll wish you had appreciated that, or something stupid like that. Then all the adults laugh. I am sick of that joke. It is disgusting. What are people trying to say? Why is that funny? Little boys will want kissing when they become men, they think. That is not true. I have not seen that. They are trying to say that men are not desperate enough for kissing to want to be kissed by you, obviously. You are being too sensitive. They do not want kissing at all. I made them that way. Men don't like to be kissed. It is not true, that joke. It is a mean joke. Men like kissing only beautiful women, that's all. God made them that way.

I don't know, what do you think happened? Well, the underwear came off, then it was put back on. Yeah, that's what I figured. But I love hearing the words, let go of my daughter. If you want somebody to let go of your daughter then you probably don't want them to take your daughter's underwear off. Unless you are saying, let go of my daughter, so she can be closer to me, so I can take her underwear off. But usually it is said out of a protective anger, a protective anger. Protective anger is so beautiful. Protective anger was so wonderful of you to think of, God. It would be wonderful, God, if you could feel it. Every time a man says, let go of my daughter, I think about how some men make love to their daughters. Maybe some of us have to be made love to by our fathers so the rest of us can be only loved by our fathers. Without meeting the people who were made love to by their fathers, how are the people who were loved by their fathers ever going to know to be happy? Some of us have to be sad sometimes, so the others know to be happy, be loved, then go to heaven.

So, my first real kiss was my older cousin Kindness. Age uncertain, season uncertain. My second first kiss was my baby cousin, the son of my uncle who died. I put my lips on his lips while he was sleeping so I could see what it would be like to kiss a boy. Age uncertain, season uncertain. My third first kiss was my crazy uncle. He walked around all day collecting garbage to bring back to our house. On one of those days he got hit by a car. I had to help him do things until he got better. I had to help him move his legs. I would hold one up and bring it down slowly and softly over and over again. One of my hands would go on his knees and the other on his ankles. At first he wanted the hand on his knees to go further up. I put my hands on his thighs because I was fourteen and it was summer. Then he wanted my hands up further. He wanted to put his hands on top of my hands. He would do this with this pained look on his face. It hurt him to have to do it, but it felt good too. Then one day he grabbed me as he whimpered. He was tearing up and making strange begging faces. He put me on top of him after months of making me keep my hands on his upper thigh with his hands on mine sometimes. I could have gotten away. But I didn't get away because he looked so sad. I thought what is it that you want me to do for you right now? All right, I suppose I can get on top of you. I suppose. He tried to really kiss my mouth but I couldn't let that happen. My crazy uncle had no teeth and he never bathed with soap. He only used water. He kissed me on the neck instead. It was strange how something so sloppy could feel like a hand around your throat. How wonderful of you to think of kissing, God.

It is something that can happen so slowly and so softly. Age fourteen, in the summer. My fourth first kiss was with the girl. She was drunk all the time, but I had never been drunk. She wanted to show me the joys of drinking so we could spin together. I ended up sharing a bed with her. Then she woke me up in the middle of the night to say that I was intense while she was holding me. Intense. Intense, that is not like being nice or awkward. I kissed her and put my fingers inside her like she showed me. I had to burn my tongue with scalding coffee the next morning. I drank cup after cup of scalding coffee so that my tongue and my intestines could be clean. She smelled bad. She smelled rotten, not like soup or bread. I learned then that kissing a girl was similar to kissing myself. I kissed the girl the way I would have wanted to be kissed, the way I kiss pillows. I imagined how she would like her breasts touched, the way I like my breasts touched, and I did that. But still it did not turn out quite right. Age nineteen, in the spring. My fifth first kiss was the drunk girl's boyfriend. She told him to kiss me as a gift to me because I was nineteen in the spring and no man that I knew of had ever wanted to kiss me, except my crazy uncle. They walked in the front door and he said I have a surprise for you. She kept on walking to her room with a sloppy smile on her face, but he stayed. He put me up against a wall and put his mouth to my mouth. He told me that I have to keep my mouth a little open sometimes. I said, oh, it's ok, thank you anyway. I said it with this grateful, sad smile on my face. I did not want him to be my first kiss. But I wanted to be nice because I knew both the girl and the boy were only trying to be kind. That's why. By the time a boy with a beautiful Irish accent kissed me I had waited so long for a real first kiss with a real boy that I understood how kissing makes love, and love makes people hate each other. I kissed boy number two when I was twenty-one in the spring. I had seen him around before in the laundry room. One day I heard him playing his guitar with an Irish accent in the laundry room. I held on to my cross and I asked God to give him to me. I went in and pretended I needed to do my laundry. He talked to me about books. He said he would let me borrow one of his favorite books. The next day he came by my room shivering and dewy to give me a book. He likes me, there is a God, I thought. Do you remember when I knew you existed? The day he kissed me we had been drinking milk and whiskey. I was going to leave his room but he asked me to stay a while longer, he wanted me to listen to his favorite song. We were on the floor listening to music and he reached out and held on to one of my fingers and stroked it with his thumb. Then he slowly brought his face closer to my face and put his mouth on mine. His two thick lips went in between my two thin lips. He went up and down and in between my lips. My mouth became a whole body that moves, that dances and hugs. I maybe should not have licked his teeth, but I thought it would show him that I loved his teeth. He hated his teeth. I maybe should have let him touch my face and hair, but I thought I was doing him a favor by not letting him touch my face and hair. I was saying you don't have to touch me and I will still touch you. You don't have to know how ugly I am. I was being loving and considerate. I was being kind. I do everything I do to be kind, but it does not always turn out quite right. Then later he thought I was begging him to sleep next to me. This made him not like me anymore. Then I went to his room to apologize for him not liking me and he let me give him my head while he pretended to be sleeping. A year later I was in the room and a neighbor who knew about love, and had been with many men, told me that sometimes we touch other people for the sake of their pleasure, but other times we touch other people for our own pleasure. I was horrified. Imagine if you had told me not to touch your hair or lick your teeth? I would feel horrible. If a boy is your boy then he has to let you touch him or he doesn't love you, she said. After he kissed me he told me that I was begging. You're begging, he said with an Irish accent. He stopped talking to me but I would still see him around the laundry room. He was tall, blue eyes, brown hair, and an Irish accent. Eventually I got drunk on whiskey, without milk, and stumbled towards his room. He opened the door and then went back to lying down on his bed and stared at the television. I sat beside him and said, I know I like you but you don't like me. He didn't look at me. I know I like you but you don't like me, I turned and stared at the television. Eventually he put me on top of him. What is this, I said. That's my boyo. He laughed. He let me give him my head. At the time I thought I had done it right. I thought this because I had water from the inside of his body on my body. Wake up. Wake up. He fell asleep so quickly. He falls asleep so quickly but he had been so soft. I walked out smelling like his water smells. I walked. I paced around the hallway outside his room. One of his friends saw me and asked me to come inside his room. I said, I like him but he does not like me. Forget about him, you are lovely, he said in an Irish accent. He put his hands on my face. He quickly brought his thin lips to my mouth. He quickly put his tongue in my mouth. He tasted rotten. My mouth could not move, it could not do anything but beg. I was twenty-one in the spring. By the time a boy really made love to me, to me, I could appreciate how wonderful it was to be a woman who knew what a man's back looked like. I knew that boy number four's back was littered with moles. I thought I could be one of those women too, women who knew about men's backs because they have seen men naked. I can talk to other women about taking men's clothes off now, I thought. You have orange energy, he said. Red is the color of intensity and yellow is the color of fear. I am not scared, I said. Yes, you are, but that's what's so sexy. You are scared, but willing. That's what's so sexy. Yes. Yes. Yes. I have been intense, and now I am sexy. I am intense and sexy. He wanted me because he thought nobody had been inside me before. He thought this because I told him that nobody had been inside me before. I didn't think that boy number three was worth mentioning. He was awkward, and he threw my underwear in my face then told me about Judy and how she challenges him. Besides, he was only inside me for a few minutes. Nothing can happen in only a few minutes. It was only just long enough for me to still be able to feel the painful pressure of having been expanded from the inside out as he said the word Judy.

I imagine taking a man's clothes off often. I imagine I would do this slowly. I imagine men naked. You don't want to get your eyes too trained at seeing all that oddly shaped skin. You have to ease your eyes into it. First, then second, and then, until finally. See all that oddly shaped skin. It is yours for the taking and having for a little while. It is all you can keep in life. You can keep skin and hair. I want every hair on my head to be the same length. If every hair on my head were the same length then I would be happy. I would be balanced. The wonderful thing about me and all this hair is that there is so much of it. There is so much of it that

115

I don't think it will ever leave me. Even if I tried to take it all out it would grow back. While Stan is pulling one hair out, the other ones would have already begun to grow back. Even when I can see the small white knob it used as hands to attach itself to my skin and I think this hair must be dead, it comes back. If I made Stan pluck every single hair out of my naked body he would have to sit with me for months and months, and even then all that hair would grow back.

Why do you keep staring at my body? A boy asked me this question. Because bodies are where everybody lives. Because your body is the same as my body, but it is different enough for me to love it. Because I feel enough. Because I am a woman and so have a woman's body. I cannot have a man's body too unless I have a man.

I imagine this man who feels comfortable sticking his fingers inside me whenever he wants to. He just comes home from work and he walks over and he holds me and he puts his fingers inside me. I imagine feeling so loved that I don't mind if he sticks his fingers inside me whenever he wants to because he loves me and I love him and we know what everything we do means to each other because we know the meaning of life. He wants to know if I am wet because it is his business, that's all. He has always wanted to have a woman's body all for himself, because he is a man, and so had only had a man's body before I became his woman. I imagine a man whispering, you're so wet, slowly and softly in my ear as he is holding me. He makes sure that he is not too close to my ear and not too far away. I would like to hear clearly what he is saying, as well as feel his lips brush against my ear lightly. But when I am not imagining I look at a boy's body and I think about how slender his toes are and how I never wanted to stare at slender toes for a lifetime. No, certainly not, I do not want slender toes for the rest of my life, no wide feet either. I unwrap this present slowly as I am critiquing it. I think, how dare you? How dare you feel you have a right to ever stick your fingers in my body whenever you feel like it? How can you have so little respect for my body? I wish it were Stan's toes I was looking at and Stan's fingers inside of me. But still I took the clothes off of men who are not Stan. And you pretend you like slender toes. Why do you do this? Because, God, no matter whose voice it is, it is always good to hear what somebody has to say about how wet you are. If you are wet in a forest and nobody sticks their fingers inside you then do you even have a cunt? Or did they cut it up?

The old man, he walked up to me naked once and put

his cock inside my mouth. He could have said, put me in your mouth, but he didn't. He could have asked, can I put myself in your mouth, but he didn't. He knew that about me. I want to be with somebody who would walk up to me and put himself inside my mouth. He just must not have known that I did not want it to be him. I was twenty-four, it was summer. Some young women make old men wish they could be young again. I wanted to make the old man wish that he had a soul and that good people go to heaven. I wanted this because I already knew that I could not make an old man wish he were young again. I was not that type of a young girl.

We are on a mission to save the whole world. How exciting. The earth will be saved from spinning. How wonderful will that be? How will it happen? We live in a world that is spinning, and some of us want to save it so desperately that we write about it and talk about it, and sing about it. The same world where the same some of us get together with our friends and plan on getting a girl alone in a room so we could all have some fun with her. Hold her down while we take turns. Hold her down for each other, because we are like brothers to each other. Watch her squirm so we can laugh with each other about it later, make memories with each other. Do these men do this because they would like to save the world, but they can't? Are they sad because they can't go on a mission to save the earth? No, those with weaker bodies have always been taken against their will, that's how I designed them. It is what women and men do to children. It is what men do to women. It is what people do to people. The weak will be taken. It is a daily war. Thank you, God. So I will wake up everyday and I will know that my body could be taken against my will. I prepare for the stares I will give the stronger person above me. It is my water. It is my water. But I will watch you. I will stare to let you know that I am willing to be the one, the reason you go to hell. You will get off of me and walk away from this but forever you will feel like you are constantly sinking. Or you can just be happy with whatever happens to you.

Christ had the right idea. He already knew what would happen to all the girls. He knew then the soldier would spill the water before the people on the train drank. When one really considers what goes on in rooms all over the world, one realizes that the only thing to do now is to die on a cross. Christ had the right idea. If you could only see all those brothers alone in a room with their girls right now. All those brothers are doing things to their one girl right now all over the world. How many brothers would that be? How many girls is that happening to right now? Thousands of brothers are alone in a room with their girls right now. Millions of girls are alone in a room with their brothers. And we cannot save the world. We cannot even save the girl. And I cannot save the world. So, all we can do is say to the world, if I cannot save you then I will die for you. I will spread out in front of you. I will spread out, arms outstretched like a yellow star on brown wood that comes from the earth. People will watch me suffer. They will watch my blood drip slowly and feel sadness and shame, at least for a little while. At least for a few minutes. Let's take some time out, bow our heads in a moment of silence for the spinning earth, and all the girls in it who cannot get out of that room because they are being held down.

My first dance was with a teacher in front of everybody. It was humiliating because I couldn't dance the way he wanted me to. I couldn't do it right. That's when I knew that being in a room with a man is very complicated. I was born seeing. I was born hearing and tasting and smelling and touching. Then I learned about being in a room with a man because everybody was watching me dance with my teacher. He picked me out of everybody standing in line, to teach me how to dance, and I couldn't do it right. I had learned some things there were to know before that day. I had been alone in rooms with men before, but that was the day I really knew it was very complicated. It became my sixth sense when I realized that it was why my other five senses were working together. I could see my teacher. I could hear my teacher. I could feel his arms around me. I could smell him and I could imagine what he would taste like. It humiliated me. Age thirteen, in the spring.

You are treating me like the people treated the people on the trains. Yes, you are being mean to me again. You have to love me as if I were your child. Love me like a God does.

What does it take to love a child? It is something different than what it takes to love an adult. That's why we don't like it when adults do childish things. But we were just children a minute ago. There is no way to know when to stop. When to realize that our toy being taken away is not the same as being put on a train. Our bodies are like our children too. What does it take for us to stop loving our bodies? When they are not what we want. If they are not beautiful. When they do not do what we want them to do? My body keeps this hair. It keeps growing this hair. I like it because it won't go away. When our children have been made love to by our fathers, possibly, in very few minutes. When we have pressed them against our cousins to feel like we are as good to them as a friend of a friend was. That's when you want your body to just split open and stop.

My uncle's cells split one day and then decided to

huddle together in a cluster. They were lonely. They were tired of splitting perfectly and being perfect on their own. They were tired of fulfilling themselves and being happy without needing each other. They wanted to be a part of something bigger. They could not have known that their happiness would kill him. They could not have known that they would die with him. Some people say you can cure yourself of disease if you want to, if you want it enough. They say you can do anything if you set your mind to it, these very same people. If you think positively instead of negatively, you can save yourself, and the whole world. And there is no way to disagree with them really. Only the dead know how much they still died despite how much they still wanted to live. The people could not have imagined the trains, so they could not have positively imagined them away. And the dead don't talk. Only the starved know how much they still starved despite how often they positively imagined soup and bread. Only the girl in a room alone with those brothers knows how positive she was that it would never be her all alone in that room. And she doesn't want to talk.

Right now, I am positive I want Stan. I want him because he can know me but he does not. Like you, God, he can save me, but he does not. And what ignores me reminds me of you, God. Because I cannot see you, so I cannot have you, and this makes me lonely.

The problem is that the God in me wants to be worshiped too, wants to ignore you too. The part of the almighty holy in me wants to be cherished too. That is what keeps me waking up, the unfulfilled desire to be known, desired, and then loved like you, God. I must not want to die. I only want to want to die. All this so I can live.

Yes, looking for a wealthy, good looking man is much easier than looking for a good man, especially if your standards for good are as high as mine. Stan, for example, is not just good. He would have saved all the people on the trains if he had been there. There are much fewer good men than there are rich men, than there are attractive men. If there weren't, then so many people wouldn't have had to get on the trains, wouldn't have had to die. There wouldn't be enough bad men in the world for the people to round up the killing armies. And there is nowhere to really look for a good man. There are men who I do not want who would kiss my nose if they found out that I did not like my nose. There are men who would lick your teeth to show you that they like your teeth, even though you don't like your teeth. There are men that will open up your legs and put their faces in your soft, wide, sprawling thighs. I do not like my thighs. Why? They are so soft. I love your thighs, they say, as they look into your eyes smiling. I love you, they say, as they slowly pry thighs open to put their mouth to them. I do not want those men. Stan, you put your lips on the ground up meat of my thighs. Then we will laugh about how when your face is there the soft hair on your head makes it feel as if there are baby bunnies moving around slowly, trying to get inside me. Remember the first time I told you that you were the first man to make me orgasm. You pretended not to have heard me. You didn't want to make me feel as if you felt you were more of a man because of it. Your father must have loved you very much.

Remember the first time I told you that you were the first to make me orgasm? You cried. I said, all of my best friends can orgasm over and over again but I can't. You said, stop that. Look at you. You know you would come a dozen times with me inside you. Come is what you called it. I put both my hands on your face and looked into your eyes. I know you would do that for me, but that means more about you than it does about me, Stan. We both wanted each other right then, but we turned away from each other and slept back to back. You could have touched me, but you didn't. Sometimes when I get like this you don't know what to do with me, everything becomes complicated. As I closed my eyes I saw our heads together, our lips up and down and between each other's lips, our mouths swaying slightly in opposite directions. That night I came a dozen times.

No, good men don't fall for propaganda on how this or that is a cockroach, is vermin, is evil. Or is it smart men that don't, or nice men, or happy men? There is no watering hole to go find good men at. The rich ones congregate. The beautiful ones wear it on their faces. So when you find a good man, and they want to be yours, and you want to be theirs, then you have to make sure you don't let go of them. You have to think positively all the time until he is yours. He is mine. He is mine. He will be mine, you have to say.

Unless we are all inherently evil by nature, then it would be horrible to let an evil man in your body, even if you are evil too. Not that I haven't made mistakes. I have done things to know what I am. I have told my mother that she is an animal who is too stupid to love, so I could be sure that I am an animal who nobody loves. I have walked out of restaurants without paying so that I know I am the type of person who does that type of thing. I am a pitiful, desperate person. I have no dignity. I have talked about people behind their backs. I have taken a rose from somebody's yard and swore up and down that I didn't when I got caught. I swore so that I knew I am not the type of person who takes other people's roses and admits it. But that is the problem with knowing things. Which came first, what you did to know something, or knowing the something that made you do what you did? And I have lied. I have lied about things I said and did so that people would believe I am what I think I am. I will make a list of lies after I finish the list of humiliations.

These are the people I have given my head to: boy number two, in the spring, twenty-one years old; three of boy number two's friends who came to my room then because they knew I had been drinking a lot of whiskey since boy number two stopped talking to me. They all had Irish accents. I would drink and drink. I would put whiskey in and down my mouth. Then they would come in the room and I would put them down my mouth for just a few seconds. I could not do it for longer than that because they did not smell or taste like boy number two did. When I am sad I put things in my mouth. All people do this, so I will not feel bad about this. Bread, or liquids, or fingers go in mouths when people are sad enough. All people do this, so I will not feel bad about this. I have given the old man my head. I was twenty-four in the summer. I have given boy number thirteen my head. It was spring, I was twenty-seven. I have given boy number fifteen my head. It was spring. I was thirty years old.

Another big mistake I have made was telling on Kindness. That was not right. I had promised not to tell on her. If I had not told then I would not have had to take my underwear off. I have had to take my underwear off so many times now because I had to show everybody what happened. That is why I try never to tell secrets anymore. I only told because I felt so humiliated banging on the bathroom door, and everything was so strange. I thought having a secret would make me special. My father didn't put me in a bathroom and lock the door when I told him I had a secret. He said I should tell him everything. He took me to a bedroom so we could be alone. He put his arms around me in bed and asked me to show him what I had seen. She took her underwear off. Really? How? Show me. How did she do that? Can you show me? Now, put your underwear back on. I was special because my eyes saw something. My eyes are on my body, so my body was special too.

Boy number two once said I was a pretty girl. He put his hands on my face and leaned in to kiss me. That was kiss number two with the real boy. You are a pretty girl, aren't you? He reached over chess pieces and kissed me. He was pretending to teach me how to play chess. Kiss me. No, don't kiss me. I might be a bad kisser. No, kiss me anyway. You change your mind quickly, don't you? He even laughed with an Irish accent. Boy number three said I was lovely and the best things come out of friendships. Then when I wanted him to taste the soda with lemonade by kissing my mouth he said he wasn't in the mood for kissing. The Irish say lots of things are lovely, I suppose. They use that one word. Boy number four said you really have a sweet tooth, don't you? You have orange energy, you are scared and intense. The old man asked why does calm return when I speak to you. Boy number five asked you do have a lot of hair, don't you? Boy number six said I want to spend the next three days getting to know you. Boy number seven asked do you want another drink. Boy number eight said you might as well walk around with your legs wide open. Boy number nine said I like women with dark features. Boy number ten said it's not like anything happened. Boy number eleven said it will only take a few minutes. Boy number twelve said I had a great time. Boy number thirteen asked how many times I came. Boy number fourteen asked a pretty girl like you. How does a pretty girl like you not go out and find some guy? Well, I am really only with somebody once a year, so it hurts when I am because I get so tight. Just use a dildo, he said. Boy number fifteen said it was all right that I had something coming out of my nose. Did you feel how tight I am? No. Well, I am. I get tight, and it hurts, because you will only fuck me one time. It wouldn't hurt if you would fuck me again. I could know what it's like to not hurt while a man is inside me if you would fuck me more than once. Just use a dildo, he said.

Leam has figured everything out. She has decided that since she will never really know the meaning of life she has to have another reason to wake up in the morning. So, she will just be a good person anyway because it just makes sense. If there is a heaven then she will go to heaven. If there is no heaven then she will become dirt, but life will be easier in the meantime if she is a good person. And if there is a God, but she is going to hell because she doesn't know how to really be good according to the real God's rules, then she will go to hell knowing that she sincerely was what she thought was a good person. If she goes to hell then she has to live with the fact that she will disagree with God for an eternity though. That's it. She will wake up everyday and try to be good and think about all the good things she has in her life. She has a room, and bread, and she can walk, and talk, and see. She has her skin, and a room, and bread. She wakes up in the morning and she is warm in a bed. She walks outside and she feels the breeze against her neck and the sun on her face, because she has skin. She takes out her money and buys bread to put in her mouth. She thinks she has figured everything out. Then one day she walks home alone at night in a snowstorm and realizes that when street lights beat on freshly fallen snow in the dark it looks like magic fairy dust is all around her. This makes her very happy. There are so many sparkles. There are so many stars on the street. There are so many people.

There are so many hungry people. So many people put so many people on the trains. She instantly imagines all the people in the world who don't have bread to put in their mouths. She thinks about how they are constantly hungry and wonders again about the meaning of life. How can she be happy if they are so sad? She can hear them moaning all at once. She imagines a little hunger, then multiplies the feeling in her head. She can't stand the ache. She wishes it was in her body, but it is not. She can hear herself making strange sounds now. She is squealing, or whimpering. She begins to pace back and forth in the room. She begins to hate the starving for making her feel this way. She begins to imagine what they must have done to deserve it. It just doesn't make any sense. So, she decides to be happy simply because she is so beautiful. She wakes up and the first thing she does is imagine Stan. He is watching her as she drives in to pick him up so they can go somewhere together. Leam drives very fast, but she is a very good driver. He sees her black hair moving against her perfect shoulders and her bright brown eyes moving against her perfect face. You are so beautiful, Leam, he thinks to himself. You break my heart, you are so beautiful. Then she remembers that she cannot be with him because the only reason he wants to be with her is because she doesn't want to be with him. The only reason he wants her is because she is so challenging. If she wanted to be with him then he wouldn't want her anymore. Right now he wants to kiss every inch of her beautiful naked body slowly and softly for a very long time, but what if he smells her down there and doesn't like how she smells? So, she touches herself to the thought of him. You think you love me but you don't know anything about me, she thinks to herself. Stan, you don't know how hard it is to keep from wanting you, so I can have you still.

THINGS I WANT
TO TELL STAN:

This is what life is like for everybody... We feel bad.
We say the wrong thing to say. We are humiliated and
so we humiliate.

Everything good and everything bad is possible. You
can disappear. Your body can be cut up into little pieces,
wasted. You can be made to feel as if you are less
than the animal you are. Your mind can be taken, used,
destroyed. Your pride can be also. Your will can be taken.
You can be made to want to die even though as an animal
all you want is to live. But all good things can happen still.
You can be given things still. You can have moments where
you are made to feel as if you are more important than
anything else in the world. Anything good, and anything
bad, can happen. All things good and all things bad may
be. Any and everything will happen to you. Everything will
happen. But most of all you will die.

Once in a wind storm hanging on to a tree when I was a
child I told my cousin that it felt as if I had nails inside
me down there, only sometimes.

My brother listened ears pressed to a door once, and
when I walked out he said "I'll kill him for doing that to
you." I looked at him, hatefully, as if he were stupid, not
as if I am stupid, and walked away. He never seemed to

care what happened to me again. I hated him. When my mother drove him to a pool party I alone had been invited to, I was humiliated. I was sitting alone far away from everybody laughing and talking. I had no friends. I was invited because everybody in the class got an invitation. I couldn't wear a bathing suit because I knew already that my body couldn't be framed. Then I saw him on the diving board. My mother let him loose. He saw water and immediately jumped in. Now I can always see him jumping off into the water, giddy, laughing, happy, not concerned with the stares of those around him. I wonder how I could have ever begrudged somebody's laughter in water. Who would do that? What kind of person are you? Why couldn't you love a brother who was happy to jump and play, in water? Why did that make him so stupid? Why did you try to make him feel stupid? A brother who wanted to laugh and jump in water... Now there is nothing I can do that could make up for it. So, I give up.

I have had fantasies. A man is inside me while a woman who wishes she could be as close to me watches us. She stops suckling and bites my breasts too hard to let me know she is sad. She is pretending to want to please me. I do not get angry. I lift my arms off of him and place them behind her head instead. My attention makes her happy.

I had a dream once. The father kisses the small of her back, turns her over slowly, looks at her breasts and cunt, turns her back around, puts his face near her ass and says this smells yucky, this is yucky. She is ashamed. She mutters I washed it, I washed it.

I know that to love someone you have to love when and where and how and what and why, they repeat.

I have a womb only good for weeping blood.

I believe people waste, even when they are dead.

I told my uncle after he laughed at me, for not having a hard enough life, that bad things have happened to me, even rape.

I have often thought about why almost every place people like to be kissed are holed surfaces where we are most likely to smell bad, or good. Mouths. Ears. Bellybuttons. Cunts. Cocks. Breasts.

My mother once splashed water on my feet to wash them while I sat on the tile floor of a kitchen. Then later she jokingly stuck her tongue in my mouth.

I want to know why some women feel nothing, and some feel twice what a man feels, and why I am one of the women who feel nothing.

My cousin couldn't walk. He was older and wiser. He made me walk naked around a table with my brother and his brother while he watched us cupping parts of our bodies to hide. He was the oldest, it was a game. Once he told his brother to lock the door to keep my own brother out, and they laughed. I felt so bad. So, I laughed too. He is the boy who said I was stupid for screaming when the little tiny crabs from the sea crawled all over me.

The first time I felt really stupid was when my brother saw hair on my body when I lifted my legs up on a chair to change my shoes. He asked why do you have hair there? I felt humiliated. My mother told him that he has to protect me.

I brushed my cousin's teeth for him when he had nobody else to do it, because he could not do it himself, and everybody else found it disgusting. Blood came out of his mouth and he told me to stop even when I repeated that I didn't care.

136

I love how you glide on objects chest exposed like a bird, the air becoming wind in your short hair. I love how you paw at me and cover me like a bear. I can see you sinewy, chasing away someone who would want to hurt me, like a tiger. You are all good things every, and any, animal could be. I believe. Or you are mimicking like a child who likes to hear roars and growls. Is it funny? Is that what happened when we found out we are not animals? Is that what went wrong? The boy found out he was a man.

Sometimes a woman does want a man inside her. When this happens your skin will feel chilly blue and warm pink all at once. The cells it is made of will become circles who open up to let the cold in and close slowly for warmth. Inside your skin there will be a trickle of thick heavy drops of river water falling off of your heart and onto your stomach. Also, you will be able to smell the smell of the things inside the things after who you want has been in a room. You will not hear better, but you will be able to turn off sound and hear the water you are made of whispering. Would this taste good? Would this taste bad? You will not see better. When you want to be held you will feel your whole body made of sand with the center caving, your chest, the sinking quicksand. The places where you want lips to press against you will feel like patches of empty cold marble, loose teeth you want to move around, the places you cannot stop touching. This is all a good pain. When you want someone to look at you, you will be able to imagine eyes on you, everywhere.

If a man wants a woman and enjoys it, that's what women want, or say they do, sometimes. The girls want to be touched for all kinds of reasons. If somebody will not stop touching you after you have told them to, you think Do I want to know if this bad thing is what is about to happen right now? So, you don't allow it to be a bad thing. Sometimes you want to like it, to try it, but then you don't, and you tried it so hard you can't back out now. Sometimes you think it really is all you are good for, so it is so good. Sometimes you allow it because you understand, you understand him. You can see the sadness behind the rage and desire to have something. So, somebody does something in your mouth and you say it tastes good because it is all that can make the situation better, for one of you at least, and then you can live vicariously. Nothing makes you feel worth being touched like being touched. So, you accept it, store it for later when you need it. Sometimes you want a part of it, not all of it, but it does not feel fair to stop, since only for you all the parts of it are distinct. Sometimes you know you cannot be taken from if you are always giving freely. Or you hope it will feel good, or that parts of it will. You hope it will make you feel better about something else, or parts of it will.

She is waiting to go in to see the king, in line with other girls. She goes in and he is sitting on a bed. He motions to her, come closer. He makes her bend and suck, but she is not doing it right, he complains. So, he pulls her up, pulls down her dress, and sucks on her breasts to teach her how. She feels loved. Love is disgusting. She has learned.

What does it feel like? Like I've never been bad. It feels like I'm good.

At first we would be this way. But after a while, we would be bored of each other's bodies. You would roll onto me, and then...

Still water is sadder than land.

All the prayers compete, everybody who wants it to rain for food, everybody who cannot have rain or they may lose a life.

You die anyway, so why fight, you never had his love anyway, so why hurt now?

The body becomes porous, not only penetrable.

It is natural to use it to survive if the body is why you cannot survive. It is natural to make something what you think it is, or should be. It is natural to make it do what you think it does, make it be what you want it to be.

Everyday, I die alone, at least once.

Someone who will kiss you, though water has not touched you for days.

My feet hurt now. I have to stop. I told you I stop when my feet hurt. I have to do something else. Sit, or stand, or lie down. Sit, or stand, or lie down. I will shave all the hair off of my body. Just need a bed and a razor and some water. Just a bed and a razor.

Stan, I am shaving everywhere because I want to know if you like me for who I am. I want you to say to me, where was all that hair that I can't see now? When you do, I will take your hands and show you. I will reach out and put your fingers between my fingers. We start with my face. Where was the hair, Stan? We move down to my breasts, which you think are my best feature. Then we go down to my stomach. You stop your fingers there and you say there is something different about your stomach. This is not the stomach I love so much, you say. I force your hand down further. You say, there is something weak about your cunt now, it was not weak before like it is now. It has lost some of its smell. We go further down and you touch my legs and my toes which feel bare to you now. You quickly turn me over in a concerned panic. You touch the small of my back and you say this is not the back I have kissed so many times. You kiss my back and I do not move. You say, see, you did not move. You usually shiver and squirm when I kiss your back, usually kissing your back makes you wild. Only your fingers will know the difference between where I am still myself and where I have changed. The look on your face will let me know that you would have loved me just the way I was. But I will be special for you without hair. I look messy now, but just wait until I am finished. There will be no hair on my arms, or under my arms. Or legs, or toes, or face, or stomach, or neck. I only look messy because I want to get it all done for you as quickly as I can. I want to get it all done in a few minutes. So you have an idea of what I will look like when I am all finished, instead of having to wait for me to shave one body part at a time. Look, I am becoming special. My body is special now. It makes enough blood for some of it to have to leave me. There is blood that stays under the skin and blood that leaves when you cut the skin above it. I am going to let a little blood seep down my legs. It is not fluid like other fluids. It is thick, dark, and it smears. The blood from cuts on my skin smears on my thighs. If I put my thighs together then spread them apart the blood makes something like patchy red quilts on the inside of my thighs. I know this is always true. I have watched the blood inside me slowly leave me before and it always smears my thighs this way. Those are times when I smell most like an animal. It always smears. I sit up on the bed to see if the blood will stain the bed. I sit on the floor to see if it will stain the carpet. I want to see if anything I am can ever leave its mark. Yes, the little red marks prove I am here in this room. If I were to put this pillow in between my thighs while they are bleeding, then this pillow would be touched by my blood. If I were to keep pushing and pulling a dildo in and out of my body until I come then I would be special. My body can do some things right, just like other women's bodies. I take the pink dildo the boy told me to buy out from under the bed where I had wrapped it in a black and white night gown. I hold it in both my hands. I put it inside me and pull it out. I see that the blood on my thighs has smeared it. My blood can smear anything now. I am here in this room. So, I hold the dildo to my chest and I cry. I cry and I cry so hard that I make funny noises. I sob, heaving wildly like an animal. And as I cry I hold on tighter and tighter to the dildo because it too has hands. They are holding mine. Now I feel better. I start thinking about how suddenly and wildly I started crying. If I can start crying wildly all of a sudden, then what else can I possibly do? What else can happen to me? And so the thought of possibilities gives me hope. I put the dildo on the bed, get up off the stained carpet, and go wash my hands so I can be happy and normal again. I only look back to make sure it is safe. Just in case we need each other ever again. Just in case we need each other when I come back to the bed. But I see it on the bed and I realize there is really not that much blood on it. I realize that if I had taken the dildo and flung it across the room the blood would not have splattered on the walls. It would not have left marks. There is not enough blood inside me, not enough blood for it to splatter. How do I find that much blood? Where can I find enough blood? I go back to the bed. I will wash my hands later. Now I need to just hold the dildo for a little while. It is not your fault. I will shave more, all the places I forgot. I feel the hair inside of me. I feel a clogged tunnel inside me. Each individual hair is clinging to another hair across the tunnel. Hair is holding hands inside me. It is making me contract. I have to go in and shave it all off. I can't just keep scratching with this hairy razor. Keep scratching and scratching. What else takes hair off?

Blood is only something red. I can smell my mother after she leaves a room. Her breath does not smell like other people's breath. That's why there is something rotten about my breath. It is hereditary. It is inherited like money. I told you about that morning that my grandmother kissed me before I went to school and a bit of her breath got in my mouth. I was ten. It was in the winter. I felt that a hand dipped in bile had been shoved down my throat. Because I know I have inherited this trait I cannot ever kiss people without wondering whether or not they can smell me, whether or not I poisoned them, whether or not they like me.

Stan, I have looked at my face for a long time in the mirror. If you think I am ugly now, I can assure you that if you stare long enough at anything it becomes beautiful. Your eyes begin to put a frame around it. You forget that you made yourself stare and so begin to believe that you began staring because what you were looking at was so beautiful in the first place. I have stared at my face for a long time. I have stared only at my lips for a long time. I can guarantee you they eventually begin to look like foreign things and not like lips at all. They become a shape you are interested in, a shape you might want to understand with your mouth.

Stan, why do you judge me so harshly? Why are some things I do just stupid to you? I know you do it because I do it too, like when my best friend's mother was singing and dancing in her car. I thought she looked so stupid. She just let herself move to music without thinking about the people watching her move and look so stupid. But then I reminded myself that that must be how she would feel if she could see me pacing to music. I felt bad for thinking she was so stupid because I knew she would think I was stupid too. Even what I eat and drink makes me disgusting to you. What is it that I have done to offend you so greatly that you will not look at me even now? Look at me. How could you not love me even now? What did I say that was horrible enough for you to treat me like this?

Stan, I could have loved you if you let me. I could

have loved you more than anybody else would have. I walk around all day with you watching me. We were always together. I put lemonade in my soda that day, remember? You thought it was strange at first, then I explained to you that it makes soda taste better. I offered you some so you could taste it. You took the glass from my hands, then put it aside and tasted the soda by kissing my mouth. It was that day that you realized how much I can bring to your life, how special I am.

Stan, this is how you would touch my face. Yes, this slowly and this softly. This is how we would kiss, and this is how we would lie next to each other. You would have just had to do things slowly for me sometimes and other times I would have let you have me up against a wall. I have pretended that I wanted the old man to put me up against a wall before, but with you I wouldn't be pretending. You would not say that I needed to move just my head, not my whole body if I was kissing you, no matter where I was kissing you. You would make up for all of that. If you did not want me to move my whole body you would just pick me up and put my whole body in your whole body. Then you would stroke my face with your fingertips slowly and softly.

The browns in your hair are the color of the earth. The blue in your eyes is the color of the sky. I know, I must have thought the sky was so perfect for a good reason. The others, they did not have blue eyes, even though they knew how much I loved that about the sky. The proportion of your hands and feet to your limbs, to your body, how did God do that? This is how you would move inside me, Stan. Yes, that is how happy we would be. We would sleep next to each other every day like you are my pillow and I am your pillow, but we can hold each other back. I wouldn't have to pretend that I am me and you at the same time, which would be wonderful because it is so hard to do that sometimes.

Stan, why don't you want me? Is it what I look like or how I smell? Is it my face or what I say? What I say doesn't mean much. It can change. It isn't what I am. One right word falls just right and has the power to change everything. The way a drop of water can fall on the tip of a cigarette and put out what would have burned down a forest, or an eyelid. There is a way you can keep me and my skin from burning and you don't care.

Stan, everything and everybody reminds me of you. I saw a thin, tall man on the bus holding his bag of groceries and I thought of you. I saw a short man walking down the street singing a song out loud and I thought of you. Everything that is good becomes you because you are so good. But right now I am going to judge you too. You don't want me even now. Look at me. What do I have to do? What do I have to say to you? I have said everything. Even now you don't see any good in me. You would be the best thing that ever happened to me if you let yourself be. You could be the most important thing that ever happened to me. You never really loved me, you only care about yourself. You don't want to mean that much to somebody. You don't want to be special. You don't want to let yourself be happy. I should have known when the tulips left my body brown and dead. Tulips like spring, I am always either like summer or winter inside.

I won't be your nice guy, Stan. Look, I won't wait around forever. I won't wait until you have tried being with all those other people who will treat you like dirt before you realize you would settle for me. You have to figure out what's important to you, right now as we watch blood leave and smear. I will not be one of those men who women settle for because their mothers taught them not to beat women. I am good too, Stan.

I wanted to be the type of woman that can come with you, for you. I want to sing my favorite songs out loud when I am happy, just for fun, going down the stairs, away from this room. I want to be gorgeous and brilliant. I wish that we had shared something special before this. What if you were really sick, or hurt somehow, and I had to take care of you? I know if you had fallen on your face and saw me wiping away your blood gently you would have me now. Your mind would play a trick on you and you would not be able to forget me. If we had met on a mountain. If I had picked you up after you fell on rock and wiped the blood off your face with my very own fingers. The same fingers that held your fingers as they felt where the hair had been. If we had met in a hospital, I would have had to clean and feed you. If I had had the chance to wipe your blood away first you would be wiping mine now. If I had been the only one you could go to after your face was cut by glass from a windshield. I open the car door and there you are gnarled, gawking, ugly like a monster, with rivulets of blood separating my face and your face.

Before we leave this room I want to let you know that in every way, and from every way you were inside me I learned something good about being on the earth. Each and every time you were inside me in a new way I learned something new about the pleasures of living. Your fingers slipping in my ears as you are trying to hold on to my head. Your fingers slipping into my mouth. Your fingers. I feel as if I can lie here on this bed forever now. I would breathe here without water until the lack of water kills me. If there is a God, then for a few days my spirit will slowly sip at the water inside my body. My spirit will in time begin to panic. It will slurp and suck until I am dry. But eventually I will dry. My limbs will spread out, brown, and fall. Then I will have you in heaven. If there is no God, then, I don't know, Stan.

Marream Krollos was born in Alexandria, Egypt. She has since lived in Los Angeles, New York, Seville, Seoul, Christchurch, and Riyadh. She received her PhD from the University of Denver. She previously lived in Jeddah where she taught one of the very few creative writing classes in the kingdom.